A hand grasped my arm.

I jerked, reeling away from the touch. The hand snapped open and I went down on my butt in the grass.

"Who the hell are you?" I demanded before I'd actually seen who'd grabbed me.

A woman about my age stood over me. She had bristle-short red hair and was dressed in a black jumpsuit that made her look like some sort of extra from *The Matrix*. She stared at me for a moment, then said softly, "You need to get out of here before someone else finds you."

Someone else? I was a little worried about anyone *finding me.*

She offered me a hand up. I stared at it for a moment as if it were a snake about to strike.

"Who are you?" I asked again.

She shook her head slightly, stone-faced. "You don't want to know."

Her expression reminded me of someone else. *Oh, shit. Darien. That's who it reminds me of.* It was the same blank mask of an expression that he wore most of the time, though this girl seemed much, much more functional than he did.

I took her hand slowly and let her pull me to my feet.

"You should get back to town," she said quietly as she released my hand. "You're missing the show." She turned back toward the wall and walked toward it, looking back at me for just a moment.

With that last long, measuring look, she walked through the wall and *vanished*.

WHAT ANGELS FEAR

A Lost Angels Chronicle

Erin M. Klitzke

Taliesin Ambrose Books

Table of Contents

DEDICATION

This one is for the 1997-2005 #Authors crew on Undernet.org.
Thank you so much, for more than you'll ever know.

THE INSTITUTE CALLED THEM THEIR ANGELIC LEGION.

They expected a few hundred children, properly trained, would be able to turn back the forces of hell when the End Times came. There would be no Rapture, after all. No one would be safe, not without the protection this legion. This cult masquerading as a research organization thought it was doing everything right: by the "angels," by their families, and by God.

THEY WERE WRONG.

JUNE

"It's so sad about your Uncle Arnie, Julia."

I smiled tightly at Miss Barker, the lady behind me in line as I waited for my bread and cookies at the counter of O'Halloran's Bakery. "Yeah, we're going to miss him a lot. But he's with Aunt Miriam now, so I'm sure he's happy. He's in a better place."

Miss Barker nodded. "Oh, of course he is, sweetheart! The good Lord takes care of his own, after all." I didn't like the fact that she called me sweetheart, but I kept my mouth shut about it. I had to live with these people, after all, at least for the time being. She paused for a moment, her gaze measuring. "Will you be staying long now that he's passed on?"

"The summer at least," I told her, silently willing my order to come up faster so I could make my escape from the middle-aged housewife with the plastic-looking hair.

Betsy O'Halloran answered my prayers a few seconds later, setting a brown paper bag on the counter. "Seven forty-five, Miss Kinsey."

Thank you, whoever was up there listening. I dug the cash out of my pocket—a ten—and handed it to her. Miss Barker was still smiling at me, almost a creepy little satisfied smile. Briefly, I wondered if she was sizing me up for one of her sons. "Oh, that's good! It wouldn't do to just…up and go. Who knows? Maybe you'll find a nice boy and settle down here! Wouldn't that be nice?"

Definitely sizing me up for one of her sons. There wasn't a damn thing that could make me want to settle down in

Andover Commonwealth permanently. Too much about the town gave me the shivers.

But I had to be pleasant, so I just smiled and waited for my change. Betsy was prompt about it, mercifully.

I didn't really want to find a nice boy here, and I sure as hell didn't want to stay in Andover. Even after fifteen years of summer visits to my father's Aunt Miriam and Uncle Arnie—and the past six months since graduation living with Uncle Arnie after Aunt Miriam died—there was still something about this place I didn't like.

It looked like a normal town.

Quiet streets. A café on the corner. Grocery store at the center of the main street strip. A church—evangelical, a blue and white clapboard chapel complete with steeple—at the far end of main street, centered on a green and surrounded by trees. Antique shops and a bakery and everyone all smiles. Just another Midwestern, semi-rural town where the farmer's market and Sunday services were the most important events of the week. Just like a thousand other villages in a thousand other counties in a dozen states. And yet...

There was something *wrong* about the place.

I was eight years old on my first visit and *I* knew it felt wrong. I just couldn't put my finger on what it was.

I stuffed a dollar into Betsy's tip jar and escaped the bakery—and Miss Barker—with my bread. Betsy gave me a sympathetic smile and a wave as I ducked out into the summer sunshine and she turned to help the older woman.

I was about halfway into my walk back to the big, old house I'd inherited from Aunt Miriam and Uncle Arnie when I saw the boy. He was maybe twenty, thin and hollow-eyed, standing on the green outside the chapel. He was staring at me, watching me. There was something unsettled in his gaze, but sad rather than frightening.

I slowed down, watching him as he watched me. His eyes pleaded for something, but I didn't know what.

"Darien! Come here, I need your help."

He jerked, gaze tearing away as he moved almost mechanically to help Susan Paulsen, the grocer's wife. She noticed me watching and waved. I waved back, lingering only a moment to watch her pile a box of groceries into the boy's arms and point him into the chapel. He didn't come back out again.

I shivered. If there was one place in town I liked *least*, it was the chapel. I drove out to the Catholic parish in Albion when I actually did the organized religion thing. The O'Hallorans did, too. Beyond them and one or two other families who went to other churches elsewhere, everyone went to the Andover Common House of Worship. That's what they called the little blue and white chapel on the green.

I called it weird. Creepy, even.

I kept walking. The boy's face stuck in my mind as I made my way back to the house. His lips formed words that I couldn't follow, movement that I had initially missed but now remembered seeing.

I thought he was saying *help me*. That sent shivers down my spine. Who was he? Why would he be asking a perfect stranger on the street to help him?

I tried to put it out of my mind. I had enough to be worrying about, like finding ways to avoid the Miss Barkers of Andover Commonwealth for as long as I decided to stay here and getting the shop back in order.

Something made me want to get out of town over the weekend, so I drove home for a couple days and reacquainted myself with *normalcy* in the form of my parents. As much as I loved them, though, it was kind of a relief to leave again. I'd lived on my own for too long to be entirely comfortable back home, under their roof, rather than in charge of my own life and my comings and goings.

Twilight was coming onto the world when I turned down

the dirt road that led to the house where my aunt and uncle had lived for almost forty years. It was bigger by half than it had needed to be; they'd never had children of their own. They'd made up for that by having my dad and his siblings there whenever they could—weeks at a time every summer for us. The house was big enough to accommodate that and then some.

Someone was shouting out in the fields near the roadway as I drove by. Fireflies and moonlight brightened the world as I glanced sidelong, out into the grass that gave way to trees a few hundred feet from the edge of the road. Beyond those trees and a bend in the road was the old house, just a few minutes farther.

The fireflies swirled around a lone figure out there in the grass, shouting at the sky. I couldn't quite make out who it was from the road. I pulled off to the side, shut off the engine, and climbed out of my car for a better look.

Whoever was out there was yelling loud enough and fast enough that the words tumbled over each other, impossible to understand.

I leaned against the car, squinting into the dim. The shouting started to taper off and I started to make out some of the words as the darkness deepened and time wore on.

"I did every fucking thing that they wanted me to, so why the hell are they still doing this to me? Can you hear me, God? Why are you letting them do this? Is this what you wanted? Can you hear me up...there..."

He was looking right at me, and I was looking right back at him as his voice trailed away.

His chest heaved twice and he doubled over, disappearing behind the tall grass.

What in god's name was that about? Is he okay? Whoever he is... I started to wade through the grass toward where he should have been.

There wasn't anyone there.

There had been, though, judging from the pile of vomit I

nearly stepped in while looking for him. That was the only sign that anyone had been there.

My heartbeat quickened.

No, he's got to be here. Otherwise he just...snuck off or something. I should've been able to hear that, though, or see him, or some sign of his passage.

All I could hear were the cicadas, all I could see were the fireflies and the moonlight streaming down, now that the light of day had faded.

He snuck off. That's all.

I turned to leave and saw a crumpled scrap of paper near the toe of my sneaker.

It was an ad torn out of the chapel's weekly program, I could tell that much in the dim light. I'd seen them before, knew what they looked like.

I walked back to the car and turned on the dome light.

The Agapeistic Center for Religious Studies. That's what the ad was for. They had a big installation on the other side of town, were probably Andover Commonwealth's biggest employer.

Come to think of it, I didn't like the feel of *that* place, either. Even driving past it was enough to give me chills, ever since I was a kid.

I started the engine, happening to glance toward the field again as I started to pull onto the road.

There he was, staring at me. I slammed on the brakes, staring.

I blinked and he was gone.

Just your imagination, Jules. That's all. Only your imagination.

My heart was in my throat as I sat blinking at the field.

It has to be. I exhaled a shaky breath. *Otherwise, he's some kind of ghost.*

It took a few minutes, but I managed to convince myself that I was just tired and seeing things before I finished the short drive home.

I pulled into the drive beneath the old willow in the yard and parked. Grabbing my overnight bag from the backseat, I started for the house, grateful to be home and looking forward to a shower and my bed.

Partway to the door, I realized the shadows the moonlight was casting through the willow branches were wrong. My heart started to beat faster as I looked up into the tree.

For a moment, I thought I saw something there: a slender and flame-haired figure, perched among the branches.

I stared, then blinked.

Nothing there.

I scrambled for the house. It took the rest of the night for me to calm down and convince myself it was all nothing but my imagination.

I still had nightmares, though, and they were filled with the desperate face of the boy on the green and sinister laughter that felt too damned familiar not to be real.

Monday was going to suck, and hard.

The first note was on a torn sheet of Institute stationary, and I found it tucked under the door at the shop six weeks after my great-uncle died.

Six weeks to the *day*.

The note looked like it had been written by a child, but the rambling was anything but childlike.

I'm one of the lost. One of the stolen. Angels. I need help. Help. HELP. Please help. Please help. PLEASE HELP ME.

I need to get out of here and I can't do it alone.

It was written in red ink—I hoped it was ink, anyway. The idea that it wasn't shouldn't have even come to me, but something about the words coupled with the Institute stationary made me wonder for half a second.

I shivered on the steps of the shop, looking up and down the street. The note was dry, no hint of the morning dew, which meant it hadn't been left on the stoop overnight. Whoever had left it couldn't have gone far.

There wasn't anyone to be seen, though, as I looked up and down the street. Just a woman reading the newspaper outside of the coffee shop a few doors down, and she'd been there when I left with my morning latte.

I gulped in a few deep breaths and swallowed hard before I folded the note and tucked it into my pocket. The door to the shop was still locked and the place was still dark. I unlocked the door and stepped inside, inhaling deeply the scent of wool and wood. I calmed instantly, the sudden tension that had gripped me when I found the note easing as I flipped on the lights and took in the bins full of color and texture, everything sitting just as I'd left it the night before.

My great aunt and uncle sold yarn.

Their shop was small, quaint, full of wooden shelving units older than I was and overstuffed chairs where customers could come in and sit for hours, chatting and knitting in either the light of the big bay windows overlooking Andover's main drag or near the fireplace further back. There had been some afternoons over winter vacation that I'd spent snuggled into one of those chairs with a book, listening to the clack of Aunt Miriam's knitting needles and the crackling of the fire. The shop, like their old, rambling house on the edge of town, were among the few places in town where I actually felt safe.

The people here were just too happy sometimes, and too many of them seemed to work at the think tank outside of town. The Institute at the Agapeistic Center for Religious Studies, as best as I could figure out, was funded by the much larger charitable organization of similar name. At least, I was pretty sure that was the case. The only people who *didn't* work there worked in town, at the grocery store, at the bakery, at the coffee shop and the other few businesses that ensured that Andover Commonwealth functioned day to day.

I was pretty sure even the town sheriff worked there.

There wasn't anyone I could call about the note, no one I

could tell—except maybe one of the O'Hallorans or Patrick Garret, none of whom would know what to do. Other than them, there wasn't anyone in this whole damn town I trusted further than I could throw them.

I'm not that strong.

I set my things on the counter and went back to the door for one more look out the front. I caught a glimpse of a shadow that seemed to form itself into a thin figure on the corner. The face of the boy on the green stared at me for a moment. His eyes begged for something as I stared back at him.

Then he *vanished* into thin air—he didn't step around the corner, didn't fade into shadows, just *pop*. Gone.

I bit down on my thumb to keep from crying out.

That's not possible. *It's just not possible.* I bit down harder on my knuckle. I couldn't be dreaming, either.

Had I just imagined that he was there? Had *he* been the one to leave the note?

Miss Baker came around the corner where the boy had been standing—walked right through where he'd been. She smiled and waved at me.

I took my hand out of my mouth, forced a smile, and waved back before I ducked back into the shop and slammed the door behind me. The bells hanging from it jangled cheerfully against each other as I bolted the door. Shivering from head to toe, I gasped in a few breaths and leaned against the wall next to the door. I glanced through the full-length window toward the corner one last time.

The boy stared back at me for a moment, then looked down at his feet, turned, and walked around the corner and out of sight.

I swallowed bile. What was going on in this damn town?

I didn't think I wanted to find out.

♠   ♠   ♠

I ran the rag one more time across the wood of the check-out counter, marveling at its darkness and the fact that it was still in such amazing shape after all these years. The counters and the shelves at Uncle Arnie's shop were as beautiful as they were old.

There had been three more notes in the past two weeks, much the same as the first, though on different types of paper. They were always scraps snitched from somewhere, though, never a full, neat sheet. Two were in ink, the last in pencil. The handwriting was getting less shaky, more legible, as if the writer was getting better with practice.

I tried not to think about them. Thinking about them, about what they said, made me just want to run *screaming* from Andover Commonwealth and never come back. It was just one more thing wrong with the place.

The bells on the front door tingled and I glanced up, blinking. The boy from the green was standing there, looking a little lost as he let the door fall closed behind him.

"Can I help you?" I asked, starting to come out from around the counter.

He just stared at me for a long moment, then wet his lips as if he was about to speak. Those eyes snared me for a brief second and I hesitated before I got moving again. As I got a few steps closer, his eyes widened suddenly and he abruptly spun and reached for the door. He was gone before I could get a word out, fled like a frightened animal.

What the hell? I went to the bay window at the front of the store and peered out, searching up and down the street. I couldn't see him.

Patrick Garret was outside the coffee shop two doors down, sweeping the patio. I headed for the door.

"Hey, Pat?" I called, stepping out onto the sidewalk. My palms were sweaty; I wiped them on the seat of my jeans. I realized I had goosebumps and I was shivering even in the summer heat. Something felt wrong, very wrong.

He glanced up, pausing in his work. "What's up, Julia?"

He was a nice guy, a few years older than me, a transplant like I was — he'd come to town two years before to help his aging grandparents run the coffee shop. They were friends of Aunt Miriam and Uncle Arnie and were among the few people here I could remember striking me as remarkably *normal* in this strange town.

Come to think of it, they and the O'Hallorans were among the few, and to my knowledge, none of them had anything to do with the Institute.

"Did you just see a guy walking away from here?"

Pat's brow furrowed. "Saw someone go in. Didn't see them leave."

Didn't see him come out? Then where had he gone? Had he just vanished somehow? Completely? Was that even possible?

No. That couldn't be possible. Not even here.

Pat started sweeping the bricks again. "Was that dark-haired, skinny kid. The one staying with Reverend Stonard and his wife."

I tried not to shiver. The reverend had given me the creeps ever since the day he'd looked at me and told me that God had a special purpose for me. I'd been twelve and that church picnic had been the *last* place I'd wanted to be that summer afternoon. I threw up on his shoes after he'd told me that. My family thought it was the potato salad, but it wasn't. It was Stonard and the look he'd given me. It had been like he was looking right through me, past the flesh to see something much, much deeper. I didn't know what it was, and I didn't want to know.

I'd never gone back after that. Thank god Dad never asked why.

"When did the Reverend get a kid?" I asked. I conjured an image of the boy's face in my mind, all thin planes and angles and haunted eyes. It wasn't a child's face, not at all. *Not much of a kid, though, is he? He doesn't look much younger than I am. Could even be older than I am. Hard to tell.*

Patrick shrugged. "Don't know. Couple, three weeks ago maybe. Haven't seen much of him." He stopped sweeping again and looked at me, frowning. "I think there's something wrong with him."

I shook my head a little. *I don't think you're wrong about there being something wrong, but I'm not sure it's what you might be thinking.* "None of our business, Pat. Thanks."

He frowned a little more, then nodded. "You okay?"

"Yeah," I lied. "I'm fine." I went back inside and he went back to sweeping.

Laying on the floor in the doorway was a scrap of paper, torn from a flier about some revival meeting at the chapel. Three words had been scrawled in pencil on the corner of that flier.

Please help me.

It was the same handwriting as the first note.

I looked out the window again. All I saw was Patrick by the coffee shop. A car rumbled by — Reverend Stonard's old Lincoln, half as old as I was. I watched it turn the corner and disappear down the street, toward the grocery.

There's something really screwed up going on here this summer, I decided. *More screwed up than usual. Who in their right mind would give that creepy bastard a kid, even one as old as that guy looked?*

My lips thinned. Maybe I didn't want to know the answer to that question.

I caught a flicker on the corner, peering down the street where the Lincoln had disappeared. The boy's image wavered into view, then wavered out again at the sound of a rumbling engine.

I rocked back against my heels.

What the hell? I rubbed my eyes, blinking.

Nothing there.

I didn't just see that. I didn't. Not again. He didn't just disappear again. My stomach twisted. I had to be imagining things. People didn't just *disappear* like that.

But then, how had he gotten away from the shop without Patrick seeing?

I shivered and slowly stepped back from the window. There was nothing else I could do.

I did think I saw him one more time that day, though, walking past the window of the shop, but he'd vanished by the time he should have reached the door again.

Something wasn't right about this town. If I hadn't already believed it, I'd have known it then and there.

Yet I stayed. I'd promised Uncle Arnie and Aunt Miriam that I would, at least for a season after they were gone.

Two more months to go.

JULY

That summer was miserably hot and I spent as much time as possible at the air-conditioned shop as I could. By the time I'd come home at night, I was usually so tired I'd collapse into bed for yet another night of fitful sleep. I'd never been able to sleep well when it was hot. Something about being by myself in Andover Commonwealth seemed to make that worse.

I always slept in these white muslin nightshirts Aunt Miriam had made for me. They were comforting, somehow, and how she got the smell of lavender to stay with them through hundreds of washes was a mystery of the ages. I was pulling one on sometime after ten at night when I saw a figure moving in the yard. I jerked the nightshirt down and into place before I went to the window for a better look, hairs along my arms and the back of my neck standing up despite the warmth of the July evening.

The figure moving past the big tree and the tire swing was slim, dark-haired, and not much taller than I was. He looked up at me a bare moment after I realized it was the boy from the chapel. I hadn't seen him in weeks, not since that day in the shop. He stared at me for a moment, then walked toward the back porch.

My heart thudded against my ribs, but my goosebumps and the prickling at the back of my neck disappeared, much to my surprise. What the hell was going on? Was he *stalking* me?

I thought of his eyes, sad and pleading, and knew that couldn't be it. Never mind the fact that if my eyes weren't playing tricks on me...if he wanted to just *watch* me, I'd never see him coming or going. I turned from the window and went downstairs.

He didn't even knock on the back door, just stood on the porch quietly. I watched him through the window as I approached, saw him swallow and stare down at his shoes until I opened the door to let him inside. His head came up as the door clicked open and he stared at me, achingly silent for a string of heartbeats before he wet his lips nervously. Then, just like the last time, he started to turn to go.

No, not this time. I started to reach for him, but before my hand closed on his sleeve, he jerked, shook himself, then slowly turned back to me, staring at me with those lost, haunted eyes. There was pain there, pain so deep I could feel it just meeting his gaze.

"I need your help," he whispered, then jerked again, turning to leave. It was like he was some kind of puppet on a string and someone was yanking on his tether hard.

My fingers closed on his arm. It was thin, bony through the long-sleeved shirt he wore. He stiffened, but stopped moving.

"Come inside," I said softly.

I had to pull him inside, into my kitchen, but he offered no resistance or complaint otherwise. I closed the door and he exhaled, sagging a little as if relieved, slumping as if someone had suddenly cut all the strings. I let go and he fumbled his way to one of my kitchen chairs, collapsing into it. He pressed thin, long-fingered hands against the tabletop, fingers splayed wide.

"May I have some water, please?" His voice was soft, as if he feared someone would hear him even though we were alone.

"Sure," I said, watching him for another moment before I turned to the refrigerator. His eyes were closed when I turned back with a cup in hand, filled with ice water from the pitcher I kept cold.

"Thank you," he whispered as I set the glass by his hand.

"You're welcome." I sat down across from him, studying him for a long moment. He was pale, though not fair, and much skinnier than I'd have expected. *What's wrong with him? Is he autistic? Damaged? Or something else? Who is he, and what's wrong with him?* There wasn't a question in my mind that there was *something* wrong, it was just a question of what—and who or what was responsible for his current state. "What's your name?"

"Darien," he said quietly. One hand wrapped around the glass and he drank deeply before opening his eyes. They were green with a copper ring around the pupil. "You're Julia. You run the yarn store."

I nodded. "Yeah. You came in a few weeks ago, but you left." *I don't think he's crazy, even though I probably should.* My brows knit. Every logical part of my brain screamed that I shouldn't have let him into the house, but my intuition said otherwise. It made a partner of my compassion and overrode logic.

Maybe those couple years thinking I was going to be a social worker had made an impression after all.

"I know. I'm sorry." He took a deep breath and gulped some more water. "I...I couldn't tell you. I couldn't ask you. Not like I could tonight."

My stomach twisted. "But you were ready to leave tonight, too, like last time." It didn't seem normal, but the pain in his eyes wasn't normal, either.

He nodded. "I can't help it. They made it that way. Can't...tell. Can't ask. Can't..." His nostrils flared as he sucked in a deep breath. "But I can't live like that. I can't be bound by them anymore. Need to be free." His lips thinned. "But that won't happen on its own. I need help. Need all the help I can get." He stared his hands, then his gaze flicked up to me. "You can help me. You're an outsider-in. You're here, but you're not here."

What is he talking about? "I don't understand." *Shit, if I'm wrong and he's a schizophrenic or something, if Pat was right about him actually being insane or mentally challenged...* The phone was three feet away. I'd be all right.

Besides, he didn't give off that creepy vibe almost everything else in this town did. That had to count for something.

"You're not of this place. You're not from this town." One hand squeezed into a fist as he closed his eyes and took another deep breath, his voice dropping to a whisper. "Sorry. I know it sounds crazy. I sound crazy. Maybe I am, maybe they made me that way. I don't know anymore. Not sure I really want to. Only been out two months. That's since I was eight. Hated it there...but couldn't run. No way out. Free now, but not."

I bit my lip, trying to follow what he was saying, clinging to his assertion that he wasn't crazy, clinging to my own intuition that said the same, that he was being truthful. "You were...someone was holding you prisoner or something?"

"Or something." He made a 'sort of' gesture with his hand, then rubbed his forehead, squeezing his eyes shut again. "They send some Angels here when they're done. To wait. Always to wait. Not ready yet." He shuddered, his next words coming out half mumbled, half hissed. "Hate them..."

Holy shit. What the hell is going on with this guy? "Ready? Ready for what? Wait for what?"

He stared at me, tears welling in his eyes. They were tears of fear, of desperation. His fingers curled in, hands tightened into fists. "*His* coming. The end and the beginning."

I stared at him, confused. He buried his face in his hands for a moment and I winced as his shoulders shook exactly once.

"No, don't," I said softly, touching his arm. "Don't cry."

He shivered at my touch. "Not crying," he murmured.

He took a shaky breath, lifting his face slightly from the cradle of his hands. "Terrified," he breathed. "Absolutely terrified." He looked up at me. "I want them to be *wrong*. I want it so badly I can taste it, breathe it, dream it. I want them to be *wrong* and I want to be safe."

My mouth went dry. I still didn't know what he was getting at, but I could feel his desperation.

"Will you help me?"

It was a plea I couldn't say no to. I nodded.

I didn't have any idea what I was getting into, but I jumped in with both feet anyway.

Even if I *had* known, I'd have done it anyway.

♠　　♠　　♠

I fed Darien that night before I let him sleep on the couch. I didn't want to let him walk home, certainly not back to Stonard. He was reluctant, but seemed relieved that I wasn't going to make him go back. I was just relieved that he'd agreed to stay, even if having someone not entirely sane in the house made me understandably nervous.

I came down the next morning, unsure of what to expect. I'd slept lightly with the bedroom door locked, but I hadn't heard a sound all night—nothing but the wind and the crickets.

He was sitting quietly on the couch, staring out the window at the leaves on the big oak tree, the blanket I'd given him in his lap. He looked at me when I came down and smiled shyly.

"Did…did anything I said last night make sense?"

He sounds a lot more lucid now. That's a plus. "A little bit. I know that you need help. Not sure I made sense of much else." *Was there sense to be made of all of it?* He seemed sheepish, almost, sitting there on the couch with his hands in his lap, traces of embarrassment and regret in his smile. *Is he actually crazy, or sane? Is it possible to be both?* I smiled back at him, faintly. He had a nice smile, at least.

He nodded slightly. "That was the important part, anyway. The…the help part." He rubbed at his eye and stood up, folding the blanket reflexively. I could tell it was just an automatic reaction to it being in his hands. He saw me watching and blinked, pausing before he slowly set the blanket down on the couch. "What?"

I gestured to the blanket, now neatly folded where he'd been sitting. "It's like you don't even think about it."

His jaw went slack and something briefly died in his eyes. "I don't." He straightened fully, looking at me square. "Some things are automatic." His hands tightened into fists at his sides. "I'm...I'm not always lucid, either."

His knowing that could be a good sign or a really, really bad one. "I noticed."

He shook his head, swallowing tightly. "I'm not sure what does it. Whether it's something in my food or a pill or something they give me in my sleep...but there's something they're giving me that keeps me...docile, I guess. Blindly obedient."

I struggled to keep the surprise off my face. "Who? Who does it?" *Shit, if it's Stonard...if it's Stonard...what would I do? What could I do?*

"The Institute," he said quietly.

I rocked back against my heels, blinking. "That big sprawl outside of town, the one that employs *most* of Andover?" *Shit, they're not just a think tank or a research place after all, are they? There's a reason this place gives me the screaming willies.* As I stared at him, I felt my stomach drop through the floor. *What if they're researching on live human test subjects? Is that...no, that can't be legal. I know it's not legal. Since he was* eight? *He said he'd been a prisoner since he was eight. But was that a real memory, or something he imagined?*

He closed his eyes and nodded. "It's...it's not a good place, Julia. It's not."

"I thought it was some kind of research facility. A think tank." *Innocuous. Just something out here because the property's cheap.*

"It's both," he murmured. "Just not the way you think it

is. Not the way they *want* people to think it is." He watched me stare at him for a few long moments, then smiled a weak little smile. "I don't want to scare you. Change your mind about helping me. I really...I really need the help."

If that place is doing something bad to people they've been holding since they were eight — if that part's true — that could go a long way to why I've always thought there was something wrong about this place. My smile matched his, weak and wavering. "I already thought there was something wrong about this place."

"You have no idea," he said softly. "There's a lot wrong with this place." He looked down at his feet. "I...probably shouldn't stay too long. Don't want you to get in trouble."

"I'll drive you. Don't worry." I took his hand and squeezed it gently. His fingers were cool, soft. "I'm at least going to feed you, though."

"Thanks," he said quietly, then let me lead him into the kitchen.

I smiled wryly. "You're welcome."

He sat down at the table and watched me as I started to cook breakfast. His eyes were on my back, on my hands, but they never wandered, never strayed. I could *feel* his eyes on me, but I didn't feel threatened. He stopped, looking down at the tabletop. He was blushing when I looked at him.

"Sorry," he mumbled. "I shouldn't...but it's been a long time since I watched a woman — hell, anyone — cook."

That struck me as strange, though I decided not to say anything about it. *Geez. He must have been telling the truth last night. Or something very close to it.* I just nodded and smiled. "So what did you mean last night? When you told me that you needed to be free?"

He took a deep breath. "The Institute had me. Still has me, a little — or thinks they do."

That's the second time he's mentioned them. What is it, really, if it's not what I think it is? "What are they?"

Someone pounded on my front door. Darien jumped about three feet, almost spilling onto the kitchen floor. I startled, too, then grumbled and marched out of the kitchen to answer it.

It was Stonard, and he looked pissed. I cursed under my breath and opened the door a crack to peer at him. "Can I help you?"

"I think you know why I'm here, Miss Kinsey. Is he here?"

For half a moment, I considered saying no, he wasn't here. He was talking about Darien. After due consideration, I decided that would be a bad idea, for both me *and* Darien. "You mean Darien? Yeah, I let him sleep on the couch. I didn't want to wake your wife by bringing him home last night. Was going to drop him off on the way to the store." It was more truth than lie. Heinlein had said it best: the best way to lie was to tell the truth unconvincingly. The man was right.

Stonard stared at me hard for a moment, then nodded slightly. "Well, seems I've saved you the trouble." He tried to look past me, into the house. "Darien! Come out here. It's time to come home."

I swallowed bile as I realized I didn't want to let Darien leave with him. "It wouldn't be any trouble, Reverend," I said. "I can bring him home."

He grunted, barely acknowledging me as Darien touched my shoulder lightly. The younger man's face was blank, but his eyes shown with gratitude as he looked at me. I bit down on the inside of my cheek and stepped aside. He slid out onto the front porch. Stonard put his arm around his shoulders and started to lead him toward the old Lincoln sitting in the gravel drive. I stepped barefoot out onto the porch.

There has to be something I can do.

"Reverend?" I called after them. "I could use a strong back at the store every so often, if you could spare him for a few hours here and there."

It was all I could do, all I could think of at the time.

Stonard turned and looked at me, then inclined his head

slightly, tone carefully neutral. "I'll talk to my wife."

And then, they were gone.

♠   ♠   ♠

The compound that housed the Institute at the Agapeistic Center for Religious Studies stood two miles outside of the village proper, off a paved road that disintegrated into gravel a few dozen feet after the turn-off for the Institute. A scene from the death of Christ stood on a lawn near a fifteen-foot tall gate that looked like it was maybe made of wrought iron.

An internet search hadn't yielded much information about the place, only that the Agapeistic Center for Religious Studies was a somewhat respected charity, even if they were extreme in their views on right, wrong, and the practice of Christianity. The Institute at the Agapeistic Center, however, yielded even less information. It was almost as if the place didn't exist beyond a little blurb buried on the ACRS's website, which described the Institute as being "dedicated to furthering man's understanding of the gifts granted in Jesus' name."

That hadn't done *anything* to allay my concerns about the place. If anything, it began to erase any doubts I had that Darien had been telling me the truth.

My shoes crunched on the gravel lining the edge of the roadway as I climbed out of the car and headed for the gate. The closer I got, the more it seemed less like some kind of corporate headquarters and more like one giant, palatial maximum security prison, minus the barbed wire fences and guard towers.

I didn't see any cameras or guards as I walked up to the gate and peered between the iron bars. I could see lawns and outbuildings beyond them. Set at an odd angle to the main gate was another wall, surrounded by trees and draped in ivy, with another massive gate that stood open. Another building, taller than the rest, stood inside that wall's protective confines, made of sandstone with tiny mirrored windows at the higher levels—and only at the higher levels. The levels just above the high wall didn't seem to have any windows until at least two floors up.

What the heck is that? The main building? Headquarters? I frowned, squinting. Were the window bigger on the top floor? I rubbed my eyes. They certainly seemed bigger near the top, but it was hard to tell from my acute angle and peering up through those trees.

A flicker of movement caught my attention and I tore my eyes away from the building, peering through the gap in the inner wall. The angle made it hard, but I thought I'd seen...

There! A gaunt figure stared at me from just within my line of sight. It was a man, dark-haired and scrawny, dressed in what looked like sweats. Though I couldn't see his eyes, or really make out the features of his face, I had the feeling he was looking right at me.

Something about the figure reminded me of Darien, but I couldn't say what. I tried to beckon him over.

He just shook his head and looked down.

What's going on in there?

Something jerked the figure back and out of sight. The massive gate in that inner wall ground shut with the sound of metal against stone. No iron bars there, just solid sheets of metal.

Whatever it is, they don't want people to know. My pulse quickened and I stepped back from the main gate.

A hand grasped my arm. I jerked, reeling away from the touch. The hand snapped open and I went down on my butt in the grass.

"Who the hell are you?" I demanded before I'd actually seen who'd grabbed me.

A woman about my age stood over me. She had bristle-short red hair and was dressed in a black jumpsuit that made her look like some sort of extra from *The Matrix*. She stared at me for a moment, then said softly, "You need to get out of here before someone else finds you."

Someone else? I was a little worried about anyone *finding me.*

She offered me a hand up. I stared at it for a moment as if it were a snake about to strike.

"Who are you?" I asked again.

She shook her head slightly, stone-faced. "You don't want to know."

Her expression reminded me of someone else. *Oh, shit. Darien. That's who it reminds me of.* It was the same blank mask of an expression that he wore most of the time, though this girl seemed much, much more functional than he did.

I took her hand slowly and let her pull me to my feet.

"You should get back to town," she said quietly as she released my hand. "You're missing the show." She turned back toward the wall and walked toward it, looking back at me for just a moment. With that last long, measuring look, she walked through the wall and vanished.

I stumbled back a few steps, almost falling again.

I'm imagining shit. She didn't just do that. There's no way she just did that. There's no freaking way.

I took a few deep breaths, trying to calm my thundering heart, then turned and walked back to my car.

There was a note tucked under one of my windshield wipers. On a torn prescription scrip, someone had scrawled *Don't try to come back here. Google Tim and Matt Thatcher.*

I shoved the note into my pocket, siding into the driver's seat. My hands were still shaking as I started the engine and headed back toward the town proper. I had every intention of going straight home.

Patrick flagged me down as I pulled onto Main.

"Big something at the chapel," he said breathlessly when I stopped and rolled down my window. "Out on the green. Reverend's on and on about something."

"You're missing the show." I frowned. "What is it?"

He shook his head. "Some kind of millennial bullshit, I think, but you should see the effect he's having on the crowd. Hell, I almost started to buy what he was selling until I screwed my head back on straight and left."

"I'm not buying, either." I frowned. "You want a ride home? I need to pick your brain."

"Was on my way to the shop. I'll make you a latte?"

Even though I really just wanted to go home, I nodded. "All right, get in. Might as well ride with me, even if it's just two hundred feet."

Patrick laughed and hopped in. I parked outside the coffee shop a few seconds later and followed him up the bricks to the doors. The rest of Andover Commonwealth looked like some kind of ghost town.

Everyone must be at the chapel. "Good god," I murmured. "Everyone's over there, aren't they?"

"Just about," Patrick said grimly. "Beth O'Halloran's at the bakery, but she sent everyone else home. Said she was getting the heebiejeebies today."

Beth was Betsy's twin and the unspoken "boss" at O'Halloran's. For her to send everyone home was almost unheard-of, since the last *I'd* known, she didn't like to be alone in the place. "That's not like her."

"I know. I promised I'd check on her until she left. She said she was going home, too, after she finished cleaning up from baking four dozen loaves of bread for the Reverend's... whatever today. She was almost done when I left—that was right before I saw you."

"Four dozen loaves? What the hell is he *doing* over there?" *That is a lot of bread. What's it for?*

"Like I said, some kind of whacky revival stuff. I really don't know what." He fell quiet for a moment as he headed for the counter and the espresso machine. "He dragged that boy up on stage with him for a few minutes. The one that came up to the shop."

My stomach sank. "He did?" *I wonder why.*

"Yeah," Patrick said as he started my latte. "If I didn't know better, I'd say he was on drugs or something. Saw him closer up after he got off stage, trying to leave. Reverend's wife corralled him. Looks like she took him home after that."

"Huh," I said thoughtfully, pulling a chair up to the counter. "When was that?"

"About ten minutes before I decided that I wanted to puke and bailed." He slid a cup to me and started to make his own. "So I take back what I said about him."

"About who?" *Oh. Oh, what he said a couple weeks ago, about him being challenged or something.* I shrugged a little. "Oh. No harm done, right? He wasn't there to hear it." I didn't want to tell him what had happened the night before. *He'll just worry if I say something, decide he's dangerous—and maybe he'd be right, but I think there's something more dangerous lurking right on the outskirts of town.*

"Guess you're right," he said, shaking his head slightly. "So did you drive out to Kalamazoo today? Shopping or something?"

"No," I said, cradling my cup between my hands. "I drove out to the Institute."

His brows shot up. "Why?"

"Curiosity, I guess." I shrugged a little. "Everyone here seems to work *there* and I'd never seen it. It's a weird place."

"Y'think so? I've driven past it a few times. A few summers back, I can remember seeing a bunch of buses pull in there, but someone told my dad to start driving again, there wasn't anything to see. State troopers, I think, but I could be wrong. I wasn't really paying enough attention." He leaned against the counter. "That was five, six years ago, I think."

"Buses? Like tour buses?" *Why would buses be going in there? There's nothing to see.* My stomach sank as I thought of the gray-clad figure I'd seen just barely within sight of the main gate. *Please tell me they were tour buses.*

"More like old school buses. The kind with the tinted windows, all repainted."

I really don't like the sound of that. I grimaced. "That didn't strike your folks as odd?"

He shrugged helplessly. "Around here, I guess you just

don't ask too many questions, especially when you might not like the answers. Dad said it was none of our business and Granddad just laughed when I mentioned it. He said weird things had been going on at that place since it went up but it wasn't anything to worry about. Folks around here are too nice to be mixed up in anything rotten or weird, right?" He sighed. "That's what he said, anyway. I wonder if he'd say different now."

"Why would he?"

"Well, they quit going to the chapel last year. Something about a big disagreement with the Reverend that they couldn't sort out, so they just quit going there. There's a place out in Albion they drive to now and they like it a lot better. Less end of the world and more salvation, Gram said."

My nose wrinkled. "I've never been to the chapel here. Is there a lot of that?"

He shrugged again. "I guess. I always used to wonder when I was a kid where the man came up with all that material, you know? Doesn't sound like any of the stuff I'd hear other places."

"Stuff like what?" I was pressing, but he wasn't stopping me, either.

He made a face. "Just non-standard stuff, and not the kind of Gnostic whatever you see on the History Channel. Stuff about forging armies to fight the darkness when it comes, about how only a chosen few will be able to fight the darkness that'll come with the End Times and only the people with those chosen few will make it out the other end. 'The righteous shall train them and transform them into the Angelic Legions as He intended.' End times are coming soon, they're unstoppable and we need to be protected. That kind of thing. Crazy stuff."

I swallowed bile. *Sounds like a cult to me.* "And the people here buy that?"

"Some of them do, I guess. Others just take what they like and leave the rest. It was just getting so blatant that my grandparents couldn't take it anymore, so they left."

"And it's always been like that?"

"I guess? I don't know, Julia. I haven't been to that place since I was ten." He shivered. "My parents have been trying to get my grandparents to stop going for years. They said it sounded like a cult to them, what they were saying. Every Easter, every Thanksgiving, every Christmas, I'd hear them telling my grandparents that. I guess they finally managed to punch through."

"Because they stopped going, right?"

He nodded. "Right." His brows knit. "Why are you asking? I mean...why do you care?"

I shook my head a little. "I drove out there, remember? I don't know why I did, but I felt like I needed to."

"You think it's a cult, too, don't you?"

I laughed a bitter little laugh. "Which? The place outside of town, or the chapel *in* town?"

"I don't know," he said as he got up from his stool. "Either. Both."

Without a doubt. "Probably," I said softly. "But I don't know enough to be sure."

Patrick nodded slightly. "Well, either way, be careful. I think we both know what happens when you start messing with that kind of thing."

Yeah, I thought with a shiver. *Bad things.*

I saw two figures disappearing into the trees north of the yard as I pulled up the drive. I watched their retreating backs for a moment, frowning slightly then shook my head and shut off the engine. Nothing looked different than it had been when I'd left this morning, after the Reverend had shown up pounding on my door.

Tucked under my back door was an envelope with my name on it, in the handwritten scrawl that I'd become familiar with over the past month, though the writing on the envelope was neater, less hurried. I locked the back door before I sank down into one of the chairs at the kitchen table and opened the envelope. This note was on a clean sheet of notebook paper rather than stolen, secreted scraps of this and that. There was no salutation beyond *Thank you.*

> *Thank you.*
> *Thank you for your offer and thank you for everything you've already done. There was something about you that made me sure you were a good choice, that you'd at least listen to ramblings that sounded insane but weren't, were all completely true. I'm sorry if I've scared you already and I'm really sorry that I'll probably scare you again later. It's usually not my intention to do that.*
> *We think Addy can talk him into it. Might not be easy, but not impossible. Hopefully it'll be okay. We hope it'll be okay.*
> *Thank you. Thank you. Thank you.*
>
> *-- R.*

I briefly wondered who "R" could be until I realized it had to be some sort of misshapen "D." for Darien. It must have been him leaving those notes—all except for the one on my windshield today.

That begged a question, though: who had *she* been? And the boy within the double walls—who was he?

Google Matt and Tim Thatcher.

I made dinner before I dragged out my laptop and started internet diving. Unfortunately, both names seemed to be fairly common and the combination thereof only slightly less so. There was a pounding on the rise behind my eyes by the time I clicked on a link for a news article now about ten years old.

LOCAL BOY FOLLOWS IN PARENTS' FOOTSTEPS

Quantico, VA — Matthew Thatcher became a fully-fledged agent for the Federal Bureau of Investigation on Friday. His parents, Scott and Marian Thatcher, worked for the FBI for twenty-two years.

The Thatchers died five years ago when a bomb exploded in their car. They left behind Matthew and another son, Timothy. Investigation into their death revealed no clues and the case has gone cold.

Timothy Thatcher disappeared last year from a relative's home in Connecticut. Matthew, 19, cited his brother's disappearance as part of his motivation to become an FBI agent.

"Before he [Timothy] disappeared, I wasn't sure what I was going to do. I'd gotten into college, but I wasn't sure that's what I wanted to do. Then he vanishes and I decided that working for the FBI was something I needed to do, since they've got more ability to track down missing kids across state lines and things like that," said Thatcher in a phone interview.

Thatcher studied sociology at the University of Virginia for a semester before joining the FBI. There is no word yet on where he will be assigned.

"He has a very bright future with the Bureau," an FBI spokesman told us. "He takes initiative without stepping on toes. We need more men like him."

Thatcher's younger brother remains missing. Any times regarding the disappearance of Timothy Thatcher can be directed to a tip line at (313) 555-4743.

The name—Thatcher—was familiar, though I couldn't quite place it. The story of that particular pair was especially tragic, with only one of the two still around ten years ago—and being in the FBI didn't increase the life expectancy of the elder brother, either.

I wonder if he actually is still alive.

I punched new search terms into the engine, fully expecting it to spit an obituary back at me. I was pleasantly surprised to find the reverse to be true, as the FBI agent was apparently still very much alive.

There were a few articles about him busting up some criminal conspiracies, but most of the articles written about the man concerned him helping people who'd escaped from cults and secret societies operating both inside and outside the US. From the looks of things, he'd helped quietly unravel a few possibly dangerous groups before they could enact any significantly warped plans and helped some of the people brainwashed or kidnapped by those groups reintegrate into society. One particularly poignant article had an interview with him and some young psychologist with the FBI named McCullough—another rising star, apparently—in which Thatcher talked about his dead parents and his missing younger brother.

"He was a good kid and part of how I get through every damn day doing this job is the hope that someday, he'll be one of the ones we rescue, that we pull out of a bad situation. That keeps me going through the good, the bad, and the ugly. It's what I've got and I hope no one ever takes that away from me."

My heart ached for him after reading that and I found myself hoping that someday he'd find that boy he'd lost. Alive. It'd take a miracle, but I hoped for it anyway.

It was dark by the time I shut things down and got up from the kitchen table. I'd half expected Darien to show up at my door again.

He didn't.

When it became clear he wasn't going to, about half an

hour later, I locked up and went to bed. There was a shop to open up the next morning, after all.

♠   ♠   ♠

The café opened at six AM, well before I had to open the shop at nine, and eight o'clock the next morning found me at one of the tables with a crawler and a cup of coffee, going over supply orders for the store and enjoying the sunshine that streamed in through the café's huge windows.

It was almost eight forty-five and I was thinking it was time to get going over to the shop when a shadow crossed the papers strewn across the table. I glanced up. Stonard stood there, jaw set, eyes narrowed, face hard.

I swallowed rising bile and asked, "Something I can do for you, Reverend?"

"Yes," he said in a voice that sounded strangled, as if it was a terrible burden to be polite to me. "You can tell me when it would be best to bring Darien by to help you in the shop."

I leaned back in my chair, momentarily stunned. He'd actually *agreed*? That was unexpected.

"Well," I said after I'd found my voice again, "I open up at nine, so anything after about eight forty-five is fine."

He nodded slightly, then looked around the café. The place was empty except for he and I—Patrick must've gone to the back room for something.

Stonard leaned close, looming over me at that little table. "Adeline seems to think letting the boy spend time with you is a lovely idea. I don't think so, but I'm willing to try it for her sake. You listen to me, Miss Kinsey. I catch one whiff of you corrupting him with your cannibalistic, idol-worshipping ways, and it won't matter what my wife thinks. You'll never see the boy again. Are we clear on that?"

Threats. He was making threats and I hadn't done anything yet—except for admitting to Catholicism.

I gave him the sweetest smile I could muster and ignored my thundering heartbeat.

"As crystal, Reverend. You have a lovely day."

Patrick chose that moment to appear from the storage room. He paused only half a beat to study the situation. "Julia? Everything okay?"

"Everything's fine, Pat. The Reverend just came in for a cup, that's all." I stood up, struggling to stare Stonard down as I stacked my papers.

"Right," Patrick said. "Well, the counter's over here, Reverend."

The man grunted and left me. I made my escape half a second later.

♠   ♠   ♠

"It was nice of you to look after him the other night," Adeline Stonard said quietly to me as I got us cups of tea. We settled down into the knitting chairs by the big bay window. She'd brought Darien to the shop in the afternoon, two days after my close encounter with Reverend Stonard.

She was Stonard's second wife—"*Call me Addy,*" *she said,* "*Adeline makes me feel like an old maid!*"—wasn't much older than I was. She had a shy smile and a quiet voice, meek and mild, just the Reverend's type. He'd always struck me as the type to not take too kindly to a wife who asked too many questions, and she seemed like she was fairly accepting of whatever her husband told her to do.

I shook my head as I sat down. "It wasn't a big deal. I wasn't going to wake you and the Reverend at that time of night."

Darien stayed a respectful distance away, clearly not as lucid as he'd been that first morning. Apparently, whatever they gave him, the stuff he'd tried to tell me about, was in his system now.

Addy shook her head and smiled weakly. "Darien's a

sweet young man, but he's got some problems. You've seen him around town here and there, haven't you? You've seen how he is."

So that's their story. I nodded.

"But you still want him to come help you out here?" She sounded almost hopeful as she asked the question.

I'm not sure what I think of that. I shrugged. "Could do him some good and save my back from some heavy lifting, right?"

She laughed. "He's good at the lifting part, even if he doesn't look it."

"I thought so. I saw him helping Sarah unload groceries for the picnic a few weeks ago. Looked like some pretty hefty stuff." I glanced toward Darien, then back at her. "And he seems sweet, just like you said, and I'm sure you could use some time when you don't have to keep track of him." *Like the day he showed up here and dropped that note in the entry.*

Addy laughed again, but it was a little more nervous in its tenor this time. "It's...not so bad, really. He doesn't wander much. Not anymore."

Struck a nerve. "Anymore?"

"Oh yes. It used to be much worse. It's gotten better since he came here."

I arched a brow. "From where?"

"My husband knows. They're...cousins of some kind, I think." Her smile became apologetic. "I never could say no to him about anything, though. When he asked, I said yes." She looked toward Darien sadly for a moment, then shook her head. "I suppose the rest of the family just couldn't handle him anymore. I don't know what they tried, though. My husband didn't think you'd do him much good, but I...oh, let's be honest, Julia. I could use the break you're offering. Maybe I'll have some time to myself again."

I frowned. *So the Reverend doesn't want him around me, but she does. That's interesting.*

"What's the matter, Julia? Don't tell me I've talked you

out of it."

I forced a laugh. "No, no, of course not." I smiled at her, praying it would seem real enough to fool her. "Not at all. Who knows, maybe the contact and interaction will help."

"Maybe," she said, watching Darien for a few moments. "He doesn't like to be touched," she added, almost as an afterthought.

"Do you know why?"

"No." The way she said it, though, simply but elongating the word told me that she suspected — or even knew. "He usually just flinches. Sometimes pulls away." She looked at me, brow creasing slightly. "He's *very* quiet."

Maybe around the people turning him into a zombie he is. I think he's got a lot he wants to say. "That's all right. I'm used to talking when no one's answering."

Addy laughed, then sobered a little. "You'll call if you need anything, then? If something's wrong?"

"Of course I will. I think we'll be fine, though." I looked at Darien. For a brief moment, he looked back at me, then was back to staring at nothing. I stood as Addy did.

"Well…just call when you close up tonight, then. One of us will come pick him up."

I silently hoped that person would be Addy as I nodded. She smiled and moved toward the door. She stepped out into the sunshine without another word, and then I was alone with Darien.

He didn't look at me, but after a long silence asked, "May I have some water, please?"

I smiled, the knots in my stomach starting to loosen. "Yeah."

I sat him down by the cold fireplace, out of line of sight from the door. He finally looked up at me when he was halfway through the glass of water I brought him.

"She'll let you help me," he said in a whisper, cradling the glass in both hands. "He won't, but she will. She's seen. She knows."

I was confused, but I didn't think he was going to make more sense for a little while anyway.

"Just sit here for a bit," I told him. "Finish the water, try to get your head in order."

His head bobbed and I smiled. There was just something about him, something I couldn't quite put my finger on, but it was something that made me like him a lot. I went back to sorting skeins for a while, at the shelves nearest the bay window.

I didn't hear him come up behind me. He was all of a sudden just *there* at my shoulder, close enough that I could hear him breathing. I startled.

He blushed.

"I'm sorry," he murmured, looking away for a moment. "Didn't mean to scare you."

I shook my head quickly. "No, no, it's okay. You just startled me, that's all." I stared at him for a moment, then choked on a laugh. "God, do you move quietly." *Like some kind of damn ninja.*

He blushed a little more, pink from cheeks to the tips of his ears. "I guess I do," he said as he knelt next to the box of yarn. He plucked a skein from the bin and offered it to me. "They taught me to. Being unseen doesn't do much good if everyone can hear you coming."

Bloody hell. "Sounds like someone was trying to turn you into some kind of covert agent."

He winced, expression darkening. "I wish. Not quite like that." He wrapped a loose tail of yarn around his finger, fidgeting. "We're covert and I guess we're agents, but I'm pretty sure we're not the *good* kind." He looked up at me. "You can't tell anyone. They'll think you're crazy."

"Do the Reverend and his wife think you're crazy?"

"No," he said quietly. "They know the truth. They're supposed to make sure folks think I might be crazy. Maybe. I think. I don't know. Maybe that's necessitated by the drugs. I just don't know. I'm supposed to stay there and wait, but there's something that keeps me quiet. Pliable."

"That stuff they're giving you?" *The zombie juice.*

He nodded. "I think she mixes some of it into my food. I think he makes her do it. I don't know. Not sure."

I frowned and he winced again. "Don't...I'm not sure Addy is in full control. In fact, I'm pretty sure she's not. I...I'm not sure. Might just be simple coercion, but I don't know." He swallowed hard. "Remember what I said? About Angels, sent here to wait?"

I remember it made almost zero sense and you were going to explain. Then the damn Reverend showed up. "Yeah. What was that all about?"

He shivered. "I'm not sure you really want to know."

Oh hell no. Don't tease me with answers. I'm already trying to help you. In for an inch, in for a mile. "Why wouldn't I want to know?"

He winced. "You really *will* think I'm crazy. And you'd be right to think it."

I glanced toward the door. I didn't see anyone, so I leaned down, leaned closer. "Tell me. I won't run away, I promise."

He laughed, a desperate, almost cracked sound. "Don't make a promise you can't guarantee keeping."

I took his hand and squeezed. "I'm not running away. Now come on, tell me."

He stared at me for another moment, then took another breath. "They're training us to be their Angelic Legions. The Institute. For when it happens. When the end comes."

Okay. Maybe he is crazy.

His face fell and he tugged his hand out of mine. "I knew it," he whispered, jaw tightening as he looked away, toward the window. I caught the barest glimpse of a frustrated tear shining in the corner of his eye.

I cursed softly and reached for him again, kneeling down next to the bin with him. "No, Darien, stop. I...I'm just...flabbergasted."

"Flabbergasted?" His voice was dull, flat, and he didn't

look at me, just stared at the window but not through it.

"Yes, flabbergasted." I sucked in a breath and exhaled it slowly, suddenly feeling like my brain wanted to pound out of my skull through my temples and my eyes. *What was I supposed to think? He warned me. He was prepared for that reaction. And I said I wouldn't react that way. Damn me.* "I just...the end? The end of what?"

"The world."

I exhaled slowly. "That's what the think tank is working toward?"

He sighed. "They're not a think tank." Frustration oozed through his voice with every word, mingled with weariness, as if he was already tired of explaining.

"No?"

"No." He shook his head. "But they *are* really bad people." His eyes focused and he actually looked through the window for a moment, to make sure no one was out there watching us, listening to us. He exhaled and finally looked back at me again, eyes focused but fearful. "God gives some of us gifts—or genetics, or something, it depends on who you ask. The Institute finds people with those gifts. Mostly kids. I guess they think it's easier to make us—them—believe. Some convert. Some just...survive." He shook his head again, swallowing hard. "And some of them don't at all. And some break and some just retreat and wait for them to be done. But they're never done with us. That's part of the problem. We're part of their plan. I'm not sure exactly what their plan is. I just know they've got one."

Are we ever down the rabbit hole now. I wished I could say that I thought he was lying, but pieces were starting to fall into place. Why so many of the people around here seemed to act strange, why there were so many walls and gates and all outside the Institute at the edge of town—why Andover Commonwealth felt so *wrong.* Could what he was saying actually be true?

I shook my head slowly. "What do they do?"

He took my hand and squeezed so hard I was all but certain I could hear the bones in my hand creaking. "I don't want to give you nightmares," he whispered.

"Darien…" *Please. Please, just tell me.*

He shook his head. "No. I know I asked you for help, but there are just some things I won't subject you to." He stared at the yarn piled in the bin. "But I'll put it this way. A few years ago, two of us tried to escape. One was killed. The other is an example of why we shouldn't 'tempt the wrath of God.'"

I don't understand…but I know he's been abused, and the abuse hasn't stopped yet. I may be his only hope at getting somewhere he can really get help. To get away from that goddamned cult they have the nerve to call a religious institution. I opened my mouth to speak but the words died on my tongue. He looked up at me, then away again.

"I'm sorry."

"Don't be sorry," I said quietly. "None of it's your fault. You have nothing to be sorry for."

"Don't I?" He looked up at me again. "They're going to try to end the world, Julia. I was…I was a part of that. Even if for half a moment I believed—and for a minute, I did. God help me, I did."

He was shaking. I put my arms around him, drew him against my chest. He told me later it was the most tenderness he'd experienced probably ever in his memory. He broke down and cried, sobbing into my shoulder. It was a long time before his arms closed around me, before he hugged me fiercely as the tears slowly dried.

I was his lifeline. There had to be something I could do, had to be something more.

I had to get him out of that town. But how?

AUGUST

Summer slipped away faster than I would have liked, moments fleeing before I could really grasp them. Darien had been right, though. Addy had worked overtime to make sure her husband didn't interfere with us. There were a few nights Darien "worked late" with me at the shop—which mostly meant that I fed him dinner and kept trying to unravel what had been done to him, though he was still decidedly tight-lipped about most of it. Every time Stonard began to grumble about how much time Darien and I spent together, Addy would pipe up about 'how improved' Darien was, how much 'better' he was doing now that he was spending time with me—and she usually did it in public, so he couldn't shout her down. I didn't know how any of them were behaving at home, but I knew either Darien had stopped getting dosed with whatever it was that made him into some kind of zombie or he was getting better and faster at fighting it off.

I honestly didn't care which it was, I was just happy he was better.

The biggest step came at the very end of July, when he started to stay with me overnight. At first, it was only one night at a time and only while the Reverend was out of town, which happened on and off all summer. Then it was two days, sometimes three, but always just when Stonard was away. I began to realize that Addy seemed a little *too* relieved when he was gone. It was just another element of my case against the man.

It was the middle of August when I decided I just couldn't bloody well stand it a moment longer. She brought Darien to the store one morning as Stonard was leaving town again, this time for some sort of big prayer meeting elsewhere. I made three cups of tea and settled down with her in the chairs near the window while Darien went to the counter and started getting ready to open up for the day.

I waited until she had taken a couple sips of tea and started to relax before I asked, "Addy, does he hurt you?"

She startled, nearly dropping her cup. "Pardon?"

"The Reverend, Addy. Does he hurt you?"

"He's never laid a hand on me." Her voice hitched in the middle. She was lying—and afraid.

But he hurts her. I don't know if he's beating her, but he hurts her. I touched her hand. "Addy, I don't think he's *right*. Something about him feels wrong. What does he do?"

"Nothing!" She laughed, a broken sound, sharp and jagged at its edges. "You're imagining things, Julia. I know you're not my husband's biggest fan, but you're being silly."

"Addy," Darien said softly, having abandoned the counter to come up behind me, shadowing me almost protectively. "She's not stupid. She knows things aren't right here. Aren't right with us, or anything else in this damn town."

She was silent for a long moment, then stared at me. "You have to get out of here while you still can, Julia. I'm afraid if you don't go soon, you won't survive the autumn."

That surprised me. "Why? Will the Institute do something to me? Make me drink some kind of Kool-aid?" *Just like everyone else in this place seems to have done. I can't imagine Aunt Miriam and Uncle Arnie knowing anything, though—or the O'Hallorans, or Pat and his grandparents. But then…how could anything go on under their noses without them seeing? Without them just knowing? Maybe it's like Pat's grandfather said. The folks here are just too nice to be mixed up in something that rotten. Do they just not actually* know *what's going on in there?*

It struck me that as a species we had a tendency to ignore what we didn't want to believe was real, and it all made sense.

People had covered up worse, ignored worse.

Darien's hand fell on my shoulder and squeezed. His voice was tight, and I hadn't been prepared for the pain I heard there. "Probably worse."

I looked up at him. He was struggling to smother a pained expression behind a blank mask. I put my hand over his and squeezed his fingers. "I'm not abandoning you, Darien."

"No, of course not," Addy murmured, staring out the window with that same look Darien got, the one where I knew he was scanning the street for people watching us. "You're going to take him with you. Take him someplace safe."

Darien laughed weakly. "Safe. No place is safe, Addy. Where would she take me? Where would we run to? No one escapes. Not all the way."

Addy looked away from me and up at him. "You told me once that your friend Ky did."

"A lie Hadrian spun to give us hope. She's dead. Otherwise, we wouldn't be here."

I was completely lost. *Who are they talking about? Why is she so damn important?* I took a sip of tea, hand dropping away from his. He squeezed my shoulder again and I looked up, meeting Addy's eyes. "How much longer before the Reverend decides that enough's enough and I don't actually need Darien's help around here, Addy?"

She shook her head a little. "I don't know. It could be in a week when he gets back. I have no idea. I just know that I have to listen, or at least look like I am. He thinks...he thinks I'm loyal and that he's in control. He doesn't know they don't have me anymore." She exhaled quietly. "I will do all I can. I don't know that you'll understand why, but I will."

I nodded mutely, reaching up for Darien's hand again. His fingers twined through mine.

"Thank you," he murmured to her.

She smiled weakly up at him. "I have to repay the debt somehow."

He only nodded. I wasn't sure I wanted to know what she meant. There was enough of a mystery for me to solve already.

♠   ♠   ♠

"Who is she, Darien?"

The dinner dishes had been cleared. He was elbow-deep in hot, soapy water, washing up as I watched from the kitchen table. The conversation I'd witnessed between he and Addy had nagged at me for a day and a half, since she'd brought him to the shop the day before. I didn't know what to make of any of it, though I believed Addy really did have my well-being—and Darien's—in mind when she'd told me we needed to get out of this town. I had a feeling it wasn't going to be as easy as just getting up and going, though.

I was really afraid that feeling was right.

Darien didn't answer me right away, pretending he didn't hear me as he continued with the dishes. I sighed a little.

"Darien."

He stopped, leaning against the counter. "Addy and I knew each other inside. Her husband doesn't know."

"That's not what I meant." Something twisted inside of me. They'd known each other before? Inside? Inside the *Institute? So she was a prisoner, too? Another one of their so-called angels? Someone being twisted by the cult into some kind of tool?*

"We weren't close," he mumbled.

"That's not what I meant." Why did I feel so relieved? I stood up slowly from my chair and walked up behind him.

He exhaled a shaky breath, bracing himself against the countertop. "Then what did you mean?"

"Who's Ky?" *She had to have been someone important, if someone was willing to lie about her. And who's Hadrian? People they knew inside of that place? What the hell is going on in this goddamned town, inside that place on the fringes? What are they doing that they steal children?*

His hands curled into fists and he shook his head. "A ghost."

"Then who was she?" I put my hands on his arms, squeezing a little. He shivered, but didn't pull away. He leaned back against me instead, exhaling softly.

The words came slowly, haltingly at first. He spoke in a quiet voice, as if he was afraid again that someone might overhear. "She'd been there about as long as I'd been. I knew her. Ky Monroe. We weren't close, but we were friends." He took a deep breath and exhaled it slowly. "She and Hadrian were close. He and I shared a room...before..." He exhaled again. "I'm sorry. This...we don't talk about friendships and caring. It's...it's dangerous. They would use it against us."

I was almost afraid to ask, but I did anyway. "How?"

He shook his head. "I can't, Julia. I can't."

"You can't what?"

"Explain," he whispered. He was shaking, now. I wrapped my arms around him. The shaking didn't stop.

It *always* stopped when I held him. Why was this time different? "Darien."

"Ridley."

I blinked. "What?"

He shook his head, eyes squeezed shut. "My name is *Ridley*, Julia. Don't you see? That's the kind of power they have. They changed everything."

A rock dropped into the pit of my stomach. My arms tightened around him and he shivered one more time, then his shaking eased. He put one warm, soapy hand on my arm and just stood there in silence, staring down into the dishwater.

"I don't want them to hurt you," he whispered, voice sounding broken. "I don't want them to touch you. I've seen what they can do when you care about someone and I'm not going to let that happen. I'm not going to let them touch you." His hand tightened. Now it was my turn to shiver, and my heart started to beat a little faster.

"I'm sorry, Julia," he whispered. "I'm so, so sorry."

"Shhh…it's all right." I rested my forehead against the back of his neck. "Anyway, I was the one who wouldn't let you leave, right?" I just didn't want him to cry. He was about to and I didn't want to just let it happen.

He at least laughed weakly at first before he sucked in a breath and squeezed my arm again. He was shaky as he leaned back against me and I leaned forward against him. We stood there, holding each other up, as his shoulders began to shake and my eyes stung.

"Hadrian loved Ky and she loved him," he said after a long time. "And they…they never cooperated with the Institute's plan for them. So they came down on Hadrian. It would sometimes be days that we wouldn't see him because they'd made him so sick with their experiments he couldn't get out of bed. They didn't lay a hand on her. They just used him. They knew what her weak spot was."

A thousand thoughts swirled through my brain. It didn't make sense and yet at the same time it did. It all spiraled down to one point, though.

Am I his weak spot?

I swallowed. "Did they hurt you?"

"Not like they hurt him." He sniffled, then exhaled. "He and I shared a room after…after the escape attempt. He was convinced she was still alive. Then there was the explosion at the other facility and I think after that he realized it was a pipe dream. She was dead and no one was ever going to rescue us."

My heart was breaking for him. Maybe for me, too. I inhaled a deep breath. His hair smelled like baby shampoo and dishsoap. For some reason, it was soothing, and I felt warm, somehow safe.

Oh god. I am his weak spot. And he's mine.

My heart trembled and I shivered slightly. "D—Ridley?"

He stiffened. I winced.

I put my lips gently against the back of his neck, then whispered, "The dishes can wait."

He bowed his head. I felt a few teardrops hit my hand where my arms were wrapped around him. He nodded a little and straightened up. I squeezed him again, then let go, stepping back half a step as he turned around slowly. His hands came up, cradling my face between his wet, warm palms. I'd never realized how soft they really were, and I was lost in that feeling as he shook his head a little, tears in his eyes and on his face.

"I don't want to feel this way," he whispered desperately. "But I do."

I reached up and rested my hand in the crook of his elbow. "You don't have to worry about me, Ridley. You don't have to protect me."

He managed a weak smile and shook his head a little. "Yeah, I do," he said softly. I stepped into his chest, letting his thin arms close around my shoulders. They were stronger now, stronger than the first time he'd hugged me weeks ago in my kitchen. He buried his nose in my hair. "You're the first person I've dared to let inside for so, so long. I promised myself that I was going to stop caring so no one would get hurt. But I can't. I can't keep going like that anymore. Don't want to be alone anymore. I have you in me now and I'm not letting that go."

I shook my head a little. "You'll never have to." I reached up and lightly ran my fingers through his hair. He closed his eyes and rested his cheek against mine.

"I just want to keep you safe," he whispered. A tear ran down his cheek and onto mine.

I swallowed hard. "I know that you do. And you will." I slid my arms around him. He squeezed me and exhaled.

"Addy was right," he murmured into my hair. "You *are* good for me."

"She's a smart lady," I whispered. *About that, at least.*

He laughed. "Sometimes."

We found our way to the couch and curled together there, me in his arms as much as he was in mine. He was quiet for a long time after we sat down, finally finding his voice after a long stretch of companionable silence.

"I'm glad you made me stay that night."

"I am, too," I said softly. I took a deep breath and looked up at him. "Do you think Addy's right? Do you think it's dangerous for me to stay past summer's end?"

He stared at nothing for a moment, resting his chin against my temple. "I don't know. But I also don't know where we'd go. I...nowhere's safe, Julia. I'd always be afraid they'd find me somehow."

I shook my head a little. "I just don't understand that. You guys act like they're some kind of crazy monolithic...thing...that can find anyone and do anything that they want with impunity."

"They can. We don't understand it, either. People... people outside suspected there was something to make right but no one's ever managed to, despite best efforts." He looked at me, brow furrowed a little. "Some of us came out of the foster care system. They just made us disappear. They're somehow...below the radar, I guess. And no one's ever managed to get out and convince anyone it's anything other than the think tank that you thought it was."

"You don't think you could?" *There has to be a way. If what he's saying is true, there's got to be a way to get his story to someone who could do something about them, who could make it stop. Someone, somewhere. We just have to find them.*

He shivered. "No one would believe me."

"I did."

"You're special." He squeezed me tightly and closed his eyes. "I wouldn't know who to tell, anyway. I don't even know what to call them. A cult? Organized crime? I just...I don't know."

I nodded a little, already beginning to wrack my brain. How was I going to keep him safe? And who could we tell? I didn't have any answers—not yet. I knew I could find them, though, with enough time.

That was limited, though, and I wasn't sure we'd have enough. So what were we going to do?

He opened his eyes again and stared at me. "...you're thinking."

"I am." I swallowed hard. "I have to keep you safe, Ridley. If I don't keep you safe, how the hell are you going to keep *me* safe?" I smiled a little, squeezing his arm. "Keeping you safe means stopping them, right? Making them go away?"

He tensed for a moment, then just sagged, leaning his head back and staring at the ceiling. "I've dragged you into a private war," he mumbled. "Ky's dead, Tim's a tater tot and Hadrian's never going to be seen out side the Institute again and here I am, sitting here and dragging innocent people into their war."

I twisted a little in his arms, reaching up to touch his face. "Sounded to me that it's your war, too, Ridley." *You asked for my help. What did you do that for if it wasn't just to get the hell away from them, to be safe?*

He closed his eyes. "Maybe it was. Maybe it is." He exhaled and shivered.

"You said that you don't want to let them win."

He nodded a little. "You're right. I don't. But I also don't know how to stop them. Everyone who's...I told you. Bad things happen." He shook his head slowly. "And even with outside help—if that wasn't some kind of lie, too—no one can really get out. No one escapes."

There's so many bits and pieces of this that I don't have. I can't help him unless I know the whole story, not the way I want to help him. I shook my head. "Tell me."

Ridley's hands came up and cupped my face. He rested his forehead against mine, eyes squeezed shut, then began to speak in a dull, bare whisper, as if he was dredging the story up from somewhere deep where he'd kept it walled off. "Before he and Ky tried to run, Tim Thatcher told us that he'd *volunteered* to come to the Institute. I thought it was the stupidest thing I'd ever heard, but he said he trapped himself there so his brother could take the place down. Somehow. He said all the evidence he'd gathered…that was going to do it. His brother was a cop or something, or going to be. I don't know. All I know is that they didn't escape and no one's come looking. Not that I know of." He shook his head a little, opening is eyes to stare at me. They were haunted, full of all the hurt and fear he struggled to hold inside, the things I'd always seen in him even though he desperately tried not to show them. "I don't think the war they started is one anyone can win."

Something about the name he'd mentioned rang familiar, but I pushed it aside, instead reaching up to stroke his cheek. He smiled weakly and I smiled back.

"Thank you," he whispered.

I didn't ask him what he was thanking me for. My lips found his before I'd thought about it. He seemed surprised at first, then relieved. When I took him to bed some time later, I still wasn't sure what I was going to do to protect him or what he'd do to protect me. I just knew that I had to somehow.

I lay in bed, listening to him breathe, gently running the palm of my hand along the arm curled around my waist. Clumsy, the both of us that first time, but it had been all right. Nerves had almost gotten the better of both of us. It was almost funny, that. We'd settled down and gotten to business soon after, giggling out our nervousness and falling asleep together after we'd finished.

Afterward, I dreamed—remembered, really. I recalled an angry, shy girl I worked with one summer. She hadn't lasted very long—quit by the end of June—but it was her name that struck me, bothered me now. Thatcher. Ky Thatcher.

Coincidence? I wondered, staring out my bedroom window at the moon. *Maybe. Probably.*

Still, in some ways she reminded me of Ridley. She'd been paranoid, though angry more than haunted. It occurred to me that the anger could've been a defense mechanism, a way of covering up her real feelings.

I had no way of knowing, of course, and no way to track her down now anyway even if I'd wanted to.

I saw a flicker of light on the road beyond the house. Were those lights on the drive? It was three AM. Who was driving up to my house at three AM? I could hear the engine over the sound of crickets. I mumbled a quiet curse and pulled myself out of bed as the engine idled for a moment, then shut off. I threw a robe on over bare skin, pausing to stare at Ridley in the moonlight. It was the first time I'd seen him completely relaxed, without the barest hint of tension in his wiry frame. I leaned down and kissed his cheek gently, tempted for a moment to just crawl back into bed and ignore the car below and whoever was in it.

Someone knocked on the back door and I sighed. Ridley stirred a little but didn't quite wake. I slipped out of the bedroom and down to the back door, cinching my robe tight around my waist.

I peered through the window and frowned, opening the door. "Pat? What are you doing here?"

"Addy Stonard sent me," he said. He was pale, maybe a little frightened. I wasn't sure why. He braced himself against the doorframe. "She said to tell you it was time to leave. Tonight. Said you'd understand, but that I'd better get over here and tell you before the Reverend got back."

"...before the...but he wasn't supposed to be back until next week." *Does this mean he knows? How did he find out? Why...why all of a sudden would she tell us to run now, if that's not it?* I swallowed a curse. *He's got to know that I've been trying to help him, that he's been spilling his guts to me.*

Patrick shook his head. "He's coming home early. On his way right now." He swallowed, seeming to finally start to catch his breath. "What's going on, Julia? The woman's terrified and I know it's not because I was there when her husband called."

Shit, shit, shit. Not good. The Reverend definitely knew something. I didn't think suspicion alone wouldn't drive him back here. No, he knew something, and if that something was that Ridley was talking to me about the Institute...well, that just leant more credence to the theories that I was already forming.

Just about the whole damn town was in on some grand conspiracy, and neither Ridley nor I were safe here. Not anymore, not that I was starting to unravel the truth.

"I don't know, Pat," I said, shaking my head slowly. "I really don't. You better go. Does the Reverend know you were—y'know what, never mind that. Do something for me." My mind was racing almost faster than I could keep up. *If Ridley and I are in danger from the Reverend, odds are Addy is, too.*

He blinked, frowning a little. "S-sure. What?"

"Make sure he doesn't hurt her." I swallowed hard. *Shit, where are we going to go? How far will we have to run until we're out of their reach?*

Pat looked horrified, but not shocked. "Do you think he would?"

"I have no idea, but I wouldn't put it past him." *From the look on your face, you wouldn't, either.* "I'm about to make him pretty mad." I turned from the door, thinking that I needed to wake Ridley, throw some stuff in the car, and run like hell, even though I wasn't sure where we'd go or if we could find help. Something had triggered my fight or flight response, and flight was winning hands-down.

Ridley was standing in the kitchen doorway, dressed in his skivvies and nothing else. Patrick saw him and cursed.

"Holy hellions, Julia. What were you thinking?"

I knew he didn't see what I saw in Ridley, but that was by design, and Ridley and I both knew that. Addy and I were the only ones who saw beyond the mask of blankness he wore as his shield, his public face, the armor he girded himself with so he could press through another day.

Ridley looked back at me, fear in his eyes. *How much did he hear?*

I looked back at Patrick and shook my head. "Just don't let the Reverend hurt Addy. Please. I'll be in touch. Go, and hurry. Try to...try to delay him if you can."

"I don't understand," Patrick started to protest. I waved a hand wildly at him to shut up.

"You don't *want* to," I snapped. "Now *go*, damn you!" I slammed the kitchen door shut with my foot and turned back to Ridley.

"We're running," he said.

I nodded, moving toward him quickly. He reached for me and his hands closed around my arms at the elbows.

"Tonight. Reverend is on his way home right now."

"I know, I heard." He sucked in a breath, fingers briefly tightening. "I'm scared, Julia."

I didn't want to tell him that I was, too. I just squeezed his arm. "Get your clothes on and throw some food in a box. I don't know how much time we have."

"You don't have to take me with you."

The words were like a knife plunged into my heart. I croaked out a laugh, trying to mask how much the words hurt to even think about. "Come on, the sex wasn't that bad, was it?"

"Julia." He sounded helpless, fingers tightening again. "If they catch us and we're together, they'll hurt you."

"Then we'd better stop wasting time so they don't catch us." I smiled bravely. He still looked terrified. My smile softened with my voice. "Please, Ridley." *Please. I'm not leaving you behind.*

He closed his eyes and took a deep breath, nodding as he slowly get go of me. "All right. All right." I squeezed his arm again and dashed up the stairs. I still didn't know where we'd go. I'd figure that out sometime after we were out of town, well enough out of town that we could breathe a little.

Interstate 94 wouldn't be completely deserted this time of morning. Maybe we could lose ourselves in the Kalamazoo or Battle Creek morning rush.

My heart hammered against my ribs as I yanked on some underwear and jeans, threw some clothes into a bag. I had to do this. I had to protect him. No one had ever protected him in his whole life. I owed him that. I loved him.

I froze in the midst of shoving my strongbox into the bag with my clothes. I loved him? Really? *Oh god. I'm shaking.* Why did loving him scare me so much more than everything else?

"Julia." He was suddenly there, his hands on my arms from behind me. I swallowed hard. His fingers tightened. "Julia, we have to go. There's no more time."

I shoved the duffle bag into his hands. "Take this." I grabbed my backpack and my purse, then pushed him out of the room. He was dressed, now, but still pale with fear. I stared at him as I fumbled with my car keys. "We'll be fine."

He nodded and got in the car, me following half a moment later. I wasn't sure he believed me, but it didn't matter.

We peeled out of the gravel drive and headed for the highway.

♠   ♠   ♠

I checked us into some motel in the middle of nowhere, somewhere between Andover Commonwealth and Lake Michigan. I was exhausted, he was nervous, and we both needed time to figure out our next move. I wasn't going back to Andover Commonwealth, not until I was sure he was safe. I really wasn't sure when that would be.

We sat together on the bed, surrounded by the remnants of a fast-food breakfast. He stared at the television. The morning's national news was on. The air conditioner rattled and wheezed, but mostly kept the room comfortably cold.

We'd left almost everything in the car, just in case. His idea. He was so afraid of being found that I didn't argue. If it made him feel better, I'd leave the stuff in the car.

"I shouldn't have had that cup of coffee," I murmured as I leaned against his chest, joining him in staring blankly at the television. He put his arm around me as I snuggled against him, one leg sliding around his.

He snorted softly, running his fingers though my hair. "You said that when you ordered it. That you shouldn't have."

"I know." I sighed deeply and closed my eyes, listening to the rattling of the air conditioner and the drone of the TV. At some point, I stopped hearing both altogether.

The sound of someone pounding on the door woke me—and him—sometime later. Soaps were on as I got out of bed, my heartbeat quickening. Ridley rolled out of bed and darted toward the bathroom as I headed for the door. Whoever was on the other side pounded again as Ridley shut the bathroom door. I mumbled a curse under my breath.

Maybe it's nothing. Maybe it's nothing.

Still, I was glad Ridley was hiding.

I opened the door to see Reverend Stonard standing there, face like a stormcloud. My heart started to pound against my breastbone so hard I thought I should've been able to see it through my shirt.

Damn it, damn it, damn it! How had he found us? It shouldn't have been possible—we'd been miles away before he ever made it back to town. Had someone else followed us for him? Someone else been watching?

Now you're starting to go all crazy paranoid, too.

"You have something of mine, Julia," Stonard said in a low voice. "I mean to have him back. Where is he?" Despite the rage etched on his face, his tone was even, deceptively mild.

He's trying to sound *reasonable, even if the demand isn't.* "I have no idea what you're talking about."

He almost snarled but caught himself, expression smoothing out before he grated, "Don't lie to me, girl."

"I'm not lying. Darien doesn't belong to anyone but himself." I barely stopped myself from calling him Ridley. I didn't want Stonard to know I knew that name—if he even knew it himself. "He's a free man with a free will and he's capable of making his own decisions."

"He's a simpleton," Stonard snapped, "and he's sick. Give him over and no one will have to get hurt today."

"Now who's lying?" I asked softly. I stared at him, smothering my fear and all but daring him to raise a hand to me. The minute he did, he'd learn what having his balls kicked up into his ribcage felt like.

His hand twitched at his side. "Hand him over, Julia."

Go on. Try it. I watched that hand. "No," I told him firmly. "That's not my choice to make."

His hand and arm came up faster than I thought possible, too fast for me to dodge. The blow landed and I backpedaled a few steps to get out of his reach and gather myself to respond—only to see him crumble to the ground like sack of rocks. Addy stood where he had been, a tire iron in her hand, chest heaving as she looked at me over his prone form.

"I smashed the tracking device, but it's only a matter of time before he gets a new one. You two have to get out of here, and fast."

My head rang dully and it took me a moment to regain my balance and wits. "You *hit* him. Addy...Addy, you have to come with us." *If he wasn't going to hurt you before, he's going to hurt you now. I can't have that on my head. You have to come. Don't say no. Please, don't say no.*

Her weak smile told me that she wasn't going to come even before she said the words. "I can't. Someone has to keep him occupied. Besides, by the time he wakes up, he'll think you did it."

Ridley's hand closed on my shoulder. I exhaled a breath I hadn't realized I was holding, relaxing at the touch. He gave me a brief, reassuring smile that slackened as he looked at Addy. "Laren, you don't have to stay with him."

She shook her head slightly. "Oh, Rid. I do. I do if you're going to have a chance, if anyone has a chance. What happens to the next one they give him if I don't stay?" She swiped vainly at tears that began a slow trek down her cheeks. "I still have a debt to pay and this is how I have to do it. It's the only way."

Ridley leaned against me for a moment, hand tightening on my shoulder as he took a deep breath. "All of your debts to me are paid, Laren."

Addy managed a wry smile. "Get out of here, you two. Get the tracker out as soon as you can, Ridley. I know you've figured out where it is."

Tracker?

"Thank you, Laren. For everything." Ridley grasped my arm with one hand and started to pull me out to the car. I twisted free as he stepped over Stonard and looked at Addy, reaching for her.

"Are you sure?" I asked her as I grasped the sleeve of her cardigan. She smiled a weak little smile and nodded.

"I'm sure, Julia. Thank you, though. For all of it."

I took both of her hands and squeezed them tightly. "Be careful." *Please be careful, and for the love of god, let Pat at least try to protect you.*

She nodded. "I will be. I promise. Now go...you guys need to have a head start. Just in case."

I nodded and squeezed her hands one more time before I let go and headed for the car. She smiled at me and shooed me off when I looked back over my shoulder at her.

"Be careful," she called, then stooped to haul Stonard into the room before anyone saw him laying sprawled across the threshold.

Thank you. My lips thinned as I unlocked the car.

"I need your pocket knife," Ridley said as we climbed in. He had a towel balled up in one hand. I gave him the knife without asking why, still numbed by what had just happened, still in shock.

He put his hand on my knee and squeezed. "No matter what, just keep driving."

"What are you going to do?" I asked him as we pulled out and onto the road again.

He smiled tightly at me as he snapped the knife open. "Dig out the tracker chip." He dug the knife, point first, into the meat of his forearm. I cursed, almost swerving right off the road.

"Ridley!"

"Keep driving," he roared, focused on his arm and rooting around amidst the blood that welled up in the self-inflicted wound. I kept stealing glances toward him as he kept digging and bleeding freely. He finally stopped, a dark wafer the size of a dime stuck to the tip of the knife. "Stop staring! Roll down the window."

I jerked and hit the button on my door console. He flung whatever was stuck to the end of the knife out into a cornfield as soon as the window was open wide enough for him to do it, then dropped the weapon into the foot-well and wrapped the towel around his arm tightly.

I swung the car onto the next exit ramp from the highway.

Ridley stared at me like I was crazy. "Julia, what're you doing? We have to keep going. Get further away from it."

"We're turning around," I snapped.

"W-what? Why?"

"Because we're going to go north." I hit a turnaround and got back on the highway, heading toward Grand Rapids instead of the state line. "They'll think we were heading south. That should buy us some breathing room, right?" I looked at him. "What was that? It looked like a microchip."

"It was," he said, tightening the towel around his arm a little more. "Same kind of thing you'd chip a dog with."

What the hell do they do to these people? I cursed and he shook his head, pressing himself back against his seat. "Just drive, Julia. Please?"

"All right," I said quietly, forcing my anger down. I rolled his window up again and tried to concentrate on the road. I had no idea how badly he might have been bleeding. I had to get him stitched up, but it would have to happen someplace where they wouldn't ask too many questions. Somewhere without forms, without identification and names.

Grand Rapids was still an hour away, but I knew *exactly* where I could take him. I just hoped Damon wouldn't ask the questions I was dreading.

♠   ♠   ♠

A few hours later, Ridley was asleep on my cousin's couch, arm stitched up and bandaged and I was sitting with Damon at his kitchen table, sharing a pot of coffee and leftover Danish. Damon was giving me the concerned doctor look he'd been perfecting since we were kids when I risked a glance up from my mug.

I sighed. "I don't want to talk about it, Damon."

"You're going to have to eventually," he said, shaking his head. "What kind of trouble was there, Julia? Just tell me. That won't hurt, right?"

I laughed weakly. *Oh, maybe. There's a lot I still don't know.* "I don't know. It might." I scrubbed both hands over my face and slumped back in my chair. "Just...there's people that want to hurt him. He ran away from a cult and they want him back. They know about the house and the shop in Andover. They know that I helped him — if they don't already, they will soon. I just had to get him out of there before something really bad happened." *Something worse than what he's already lived through — worse than what he's let me piece together.*

"A cult?" Damon frowned darkly, then sighed, shaking his head. "How did you get yourself mixed up in something like that, Julia?"

"You wouldn't believe me if I told you, Damon," I said

with a weak smile. *Most of Andover Commonwealth is part of it. Would you believe that? It certainly doesn't look like Jonestown.*

"Try me," he suggested, tone dry.

I shrugged. "All right." I took a long swallow of coffee. "It was because of Reverend Stonard."

"The creepy guy that you puked on when you were twelve?"

I nodded. "Yeah, that's the one. He's the one I helped Ridley escape from."

"You're right, I don't believe you."

I smiled weakly. "See? Told you that you wouldn't believe me." I sighed a little and shook my head, glancing toward the couch and Ridley. He was fast asleep, relaxed like he had been in my bed the night before, probably because he was just so wrung-out after the day we'd had. "It's true, though. That's where I got the bruise on my jaw." Damon had asked about it earlier. Stonard's backhand had left a mark after all. "We stopped at a motel this morning and he caught up with us. We barely got away." *Probably wouldn't have if Addy hadn't stepped in. She talked about debts...I wonder if Ridley would tell me if I asked.* "Ridley said they'd had him since he was eight years old. I don't know what they did to him, but I know it's damaged him."

Damon shook his head, looking bewildered. "You've got to be pulling my leg, Jules."

"I wish I wasn't." *I wish whatever Ridley went through wasn't real. But I know it was. How else would he have had that tracking chip in his arm? How else would he have gone from crazy to almost normal in hours, sometimes minutes?* No. Whatever had happened to him was real. "There's something not right in Andover Commonwealth, Damon. It's not just my paranoia talking, there's something *really* not right there. The Reverend chasing us to bring Ridley back proves it."

Damon frowned for a moment, then stood up from the table and headed for the phone. I blinked, watching him.

"What're you doing?"

"Calling Matthew."

"Who's Matthew?" My stomach twisted. We didn't need anyone knowing about us, not until I found way to keep Ridley safe from the people chasing him—chasing *us*.

"An old friend. He's with the FBI, investigates cults and crap like this." He was already dialing the phone.

The twisting became knots and my hands tightened around my coffee mug. "Are you sure that's a good idea?"

"Why wouldn't it be, Jules?"

I shook my head slightly. "I don't know, Damon. I just know that he's afraid and doesn't know who he can trust. Maybe no one. My involvement in his escape puts me in danger, too, I think—he thinks so, anyway. Besides, how do you know that this Matthew's going to believe us? You don't believe me and I've barely told you anything." *You probably think he's crazy, and that I'm cracked for helping him. I guess I wouldn't blame you for it.*

Damon shook his head, lifting the phone to his ear. "Matthew's more willing than I am to believe. Trust me."

I almost asked why, then decided I didn't want to know. I just got up from the table and went over to the couch where Ridley was asleep.

He came awake as soon as I sat down with him, starting to sit up before falling back again with a groan. I smiled weakly at him and his brows knit. "What's wrong?" he mumbled, still waking up.

God, how doe she know me so well already? I shook my head. "I told Damon a cult had you."

"That's pretty much what they are," Ridley mumbled, rubbing his eyes with his good hand.

"I know. But now he's calling a friend with the FBI that I guess deals with cults and stuff."

Ridley winced, shifting on the couch. "Are we sure that he's...I don't know. Safe?"

Not somehow mixed up with them? No. All I've got is Damon and his gut and the fact that this guy is his friend. "He's Damon's friend, and Damon wouldn't get mixed up in anything like that."

"You're sure?" He sounded too tired to be afraid, but his eyes were nervous—very nervous. I took his hand and squeezed.

"He's my cousin, Ridley. I trusted him enough to bring you here. I think we can trust him a little further." I ruffled his hair a little, trying to be reassuring. He just smiled a little at me and squeezed my hand back.

"I guess I'll just have to trust him, too, then," he murmured, closing his eyes. I leaned down and kissed his forehead.

"He all right?" Damon asked quietly. He was off the phone, now, and standing a few feet away.

I nodded a little and kept ruffling Ridley's hair. He sighed quietly as he drifted back to sleep.

"We're both tired," I said softly. "It's been a long day."

Damon nodded slightly and cleared his throat. "Matthew'll be here in forty-five."

"All right. You don't mind if I steal half an hour of sleep, do you?"

He shook his head. "No, go ahead. You want to use my bed?"

"The chair's fine." I gestured to an overstuffed easy chair that he'd inherited from our maternal grandmother. Damon got me a blanket as I fell into the chair, tucking my legs up beneath me. I smiled up at him as he unfolded it and handed it over. "Promise me you won't let him take us anywhere against our will?"

Damon laughed as if he thought that was an impossibility, but he nodded anyway. "I promise."

I wrapped the blanket around myself and curled into a ball. "I'm not kidding, Damon."

"I know it, Jules." He leaned in and dropped a kiss on my head. "But Matthew's not going to do anything to either of you except talk with you. I promise."

I nodded and snuggled into the chair. It smelled of cloves and incense, like our grandmother's house.

A few minutes later, I was asleep.

♠   ♠   ♠

Someone knocked at the door at least an hour later and I jerked awake at the sound. Ridley was still out like a light, snoring softly as Damon headed to answer the door. I started to get up, rubbing my eyes as he let a man I thought I knew into the apartment, trailed by a girl with short-cut dark hair. Damon waved for both of them to come in, then gestured toward me. "This is my cousin Julia. Not sure if you remember her, Matthew."

"Vaguely," the man said, smiling. He extended his hand to me and I took it, shaking it firmly. It's nice to see you again, Julia." He gestured to the woman in his shadow. "My cousin, Ky."

I realized about half a minute later that I recognized her as the angry, hurting girl I'd worked with that long-ago summer. Recognition flickered in her eyes as she shook my hand. "...I know you."

"I know you, too, but I can't quite remember where from." She seemed like she'd changed a lot—part of it growing up, but part of it also seemed to be letting go of the pain, anger and fear I remembered in her.

"We worked together." I released her hand and stood up as she colored slightly, shaking her head a little.

"That's right. I'm sorry. That was a bad time for me."

I noticed then, I just didn't realize it. I smiled at her. "We all have our moments." I sat back down on the edge of the couch, reaching for Ridley's shoulder so I could shake him awake. He'd rolled toward the back of the couch sometime while I was asleep, his back to the rest of the room and his injured arm cradled against his stomach.

Damon and Matthew exchanged a look. Damon cleared

his throat. "They really need to talk to you, man."

I smiled weakly up at Matthew. "Hopefully, you can help us. Damon said you might be able to."

I touched Ridley's shoulder and he startled awake at my touch, sucking in a breath and starting to roll onto his back—my knee was the only thing that kept him from falling right off the couch.

"What's the—" He cut himself off, going pale as he looked past me toward Matthew and Ky. He sat up quickly, then groaned, pressing his good hand over his eyes and wavering dizzily. I put an arm around his shoulders to steady him.

Standing in front of us, Ky had gone as pale as he had, her eyes widening slightly. She groped her way to the chair I'd slept in, looking like she'd seen a ghost.

"You're supposed to be dead," they said in the same breath.

They know each other. Goddamn.

Ky leaned forward. "I thought you'd all died. All been killed."

Ridley shook his head, fingers tightening on my arm as he squeezed his eyes shut. I drew him against my side, putting my arm around his shoulder and hugging him close. His gaze never wavered from Ky. "No," he said hoarsely, "but I wish I was, now. Jesus pancake flipping zombie Christ on a pogo stick. Hadrian, forgive me." His chest heaved for a moment, as if he was choking on a sob, then he leaned forward, burying his face in his hands. "*Hadrian,*" he moaned. "Forgive me. Oh, god, Hadrian, forgive me."

"Ridley?" Her voice shook, fearful and childlike.

Matthew came up behind her and put his hands on her shoulders, which did nothing to quell her sudden trembling.

She swallowed twice before she managed to ask, "Ridley, is he alive?"

Ridley looked up at her even as I held him tighter. He nodded a little. "Four months ago, at least, when they cut me loose."

That seemed to set her back against her proverbial heels. "They let you go?"

He flinched. "Not...really. Kind of. I 'graduated.' They sent me to someone. To watch me, to wait. They were finished with me until the end, when they were ready to use me." She squeezed her eyes shut and his gaze flicked to me for a moment, then back to her. "That's how I got out of there. Then Julia got me away."

She opened her eyes, staring at me for a long moment, almost as if she was taking my measure. I looked away and bit my lip, focusing on Ridley. *Don't worry about anything else right now. He's the one who needs you. Just him. No one else.*

He took a deep breath and steadied for a moment. "They told us you were dead."

Ky shook her head slowly, wetting her lips before she spoke, traces of bitterness lacing her words. "They didn't want any of you to have any hope." Her hands curled into fists and for a moment I thought she was going to hit something. "Damn it all."

Ridley leaned against me, no longer shaking, simply tired. "I'm sorry, Ky," he said softly. "I'm so sorry."

She sighed. "Oh, Ridley. No, don't be sorry. Please, don't be sorry."

I was glad she'd said it. He was carrying around enough guilt already, guilt I couldn't understand because he was too afraid to talk about whatever had happened inside those brick and stone walls of the Institute, too afraid of what they'd do to me if they learned he'd told me anything. I stroked his hair and kissed his ear gently. For a moment, his eyes slid closed and he steadied a little more, shoulders slumping.

Ky stared at us for a long moment before she asked softly, "What happened to your arm?"

He shook his head a little, anger creeping into his voice. "They microchipped me, Ky. Like a fucking animal. They microchipped me so they could find me if I ran. I dug it out, threw it out the car window."

Damon stared at me, a mix of shock and outrage coloring his expression. I shook my head a little. I hadn't told him the truth about Ridley's arm, after all, because I didn't think he'd believe me.

"Where?" Ky asked, sounding breathless.

I opened my mouth to answer. Ridley interrupted me.

"The only installation I know about is outside of Andover Commonwealth. He might still be there. I don't know."

"I need a map." She looked up at Matthew, who blinked. "You can't be serious."

Her lips curled back in a snarl. "I thought he was *dead*, Matthew! Get me a damn map. You want to take them down as much as I do."

He winced and turned away, leaving the apartment. Ridley swallowed hard and shuddered a little. I slowly slid both arms around him, and he leaned into me even as he stared at Ky.

"He wasn't good the last time I saw him, Ky."

She laughed a bitter, weak laugh. "He hasn't been good for ten years, Ridley. But you're telling me he even might be alive and that means *everything* to me. Everything."

So she's the one that's supposed to be dead, but she actually managed to escape. Was she supposed to come back for them? I frowned a little, hiding the expression behind Ridley's ear for a moment before I could school my expression into something more neutral. *If they've got the means to shut whatever this is down...then I owe it to him to show them where they can find it.*

Matthew came back with the map and spread it on the coffee table. I let go of Ridley, edging forward on the couch a little and looking at my cousin. "Get me a pencil?"

He nodded and threw a nervous glance at Matthew, who sighed and looked at Ky while Damon walked back into the kitchen.

"What're you planning to do once they tell you, Ky?"

"I haven't thought that far ahead. But it's a place for both of us to start from."

Damon brought me a pencil and I started searching for Andover Commonwealth's basic location on the map. I didn't dare look up from my hunting as I spoke. "The village is pretty creepy. Thought so since I was a kid. Everything Ridley's told me kind of makes the general creepiness make more sense. I think they've been in the area for a long time."

"What are the internal defenses like?" Ky asked, looking at Ridley.

He winced a little. "Not sure if they're one-way, but someone like you or me can't get through the exterior walls without someone opening a gap for us. Doesn't matter for most, but enough..." his voice trailed away. "You're thinking about going in there."

"I can't let him stay there, Ridley. I only stopped trying to find him because I thought he was dead, just like I thought all the rest of you were gone, when they blew the place. I haven't been able to *touch* him since then."

Something about the way she said *touch* told me it wasn't touching in any sort of physical sense. I looked at Ridley as I made a mark on the map where Andover Commonwealth should be. *He said people like you and I to her. What does that mean?* I still wasn't quite sure why they wanted him, why he was so valuable—what made him a part of their so-called Angelic Legions? I still didn't know, didn't quite understand it all. Then again, I still wasn't sure I wanted to.

I set the pencil down. "This is where it should be."

Ky turned the map around and stared at it for a moment, exhaling sharply. "That's not so far."

I shook my head. "They think we headed south, I hope. The one who had Ridley came after us."

"I'm not surprised," Ky said grimly, looking toward Matthew. "Is there anything you can do?"

He frowned a little. "Not tonight, but in the morning, maybe. Are you two staying here tonight?"

I nodded. "We really don't have anywhere else to go." I

glanced at Damon. "I really don't think he's going to make us sleep in my car. At least I hope not."

Damon shook his head. "You can stay here as long as you need to."

I smiled up at him. "Thanks, Damon."

He just nodded, then went into the kitchen and dragged two chairs out into the living room. He sat down in one and Matthew spun the second around and sat in it backwards, arms along the top rung. Ky just kept staring at Ridley.

I squeezed him gently and he took a deep breath, giving me a quick smile before he looked at her again.

"You're going to go after him, aren't you Ky?"

She drew herself up straighter, nodding slowly. "If it's possible for me to, yeah, I am. I'm not going to break my promise again."

A faint shudder ran through him and I shifted my arm up, wrapping it around his shoulders. He shook his head slightly. "Then you really *did* try to get to us. You've been alive and looking and trying to get to us all this time."

I brushed my lips against his jaw. *I don't even know half of what any of this is all about, but I know if he was stuck there again, I'd come after him. No one deserves what I saw in there.* One glimpse was enough.

He kept talking as she nodded. "I hope you can get to him before they move him or do something stupid. I owe him a huge apology."

Was he the one I saw, I wonder? The one who shook his head at me before the gates closed? I chewed the inside of my lip, hanging onto him tightly. I could feel how much *she* hurt, and I didn't want to ever experience that myself.

I watched as she reached across the table and took his hand, fingers tightening around his. Even though her smile was forced, I could tell it was real. "You'll get the chance, Rid."

He smiled back weakly and gave her a little nod. "I wish I could help you." I heard a faint tremor in his voice, the same kind of tremor I'd heard when he said I didn't need to take him with me when I ran from Andover. "But I'm…I'm scared, Ky."

Oh, Ridley. You've got every right to be. I'm pretty sure we're all terrified here. I know I am, for both of us. It was mostly for him, though. I could only imagine how much he'd suffered, what he'd actually gone through.

The haunted eyes of the boy I'd seen—could that have been Hadrian?—came back to me in a heartbeat, along with the pain in Addy's eyes, and the look the girl outside the gates had given me.

No. I wasn't ever going to let him go back there. Not if I had a choice in the matter. I was ready to fight like hell, if that's what it took.

"It's all right," she said. "Matthew'll find a way to make you safe. Once you're out, and free, there's no going back. They don't own you anymore."

Another shudder went through him. "They still do," he murmured. "But not for much longer." He looked at me and straightened up, leaning back into my embrace. Some tension I hadn't noticed drained out of me and I held him a little tighter.

"There's so much to tell you, Ky," he said quietly.

She straightened up as well, giving us both a brave smile. "We'll have plenty of time, Ridley. I promise."

I hope so. God, I hope so.

"I'm not going to ask you to do anything more than you've already done for me, Julia," Ridley whispered softly, perched on the edge of the bed in my cousin's spare bedroom.

I tugged my tank the rest of the way down before I turned toward him, brows knitting. "What do you mean? We're in this together. I'm not going to let anything else happen to you. I promised."

"I just…" He sighed softly as I sank down next to him on the bed and put my arms around him. He rested his head against mine, squeezing his eyes shut. I started to rub his back. "I love you, Julia, and I don't want anything to happen to you because of me. It's not your fight."

"Yeah it is," I said. "It became my fight the minute I decided to let you into my house. You asked for my help to get away. Now you're away, but you said yourself that they still have a piece of you. My job's not done until you have *all* of yourself again." *Maybe not even then.*

"They're going to come after you now, if she hasn't made the Reverend forget. They know you helped me."

I shook my head slightly, wincing at the pain and regret in his voice. "I made a choice and I don't regret it. It's you and me, *our* fight now. You're not alone anymore." I kissed his temple lightly. "It's going to be okay. We're in this together."

His voice came as a bare whisper as his arms slid slowly around my waist. "To the end?"

"To the end and all the way back again," I whispered back. "Now let's go to sleep. Tomorrow's going to be a busy day, right?"

"Sleep? It's early yet."

It wasn't early—it was nearly two AM—but he winked at me and I laughed as I lay back, glad to see the spark of life flooding back into him. "Well, maybe in an hour or two."

"It'll be better this time."

"Promise?" I said as he joined me.

He smiled that shy, beautiful smile that made me fall in love with him. "Promise. There's nothing left to lose."

Nothing left to lose and everything to gain.

Whatever hell the morning brought, we'd face it together, and take it all one day at a time.

Acknowledgements

If it takes a village to raise a child, it takes about the same amount of people to write a novel (or a novella, in this case). First and foremost, I have to thank the folks I live with, namely my family, who lived with me while I was writing this work and my former roommates from Laker Village, Jennie and Jill, who lived with me when I was crafting the universe. Finally, have certainly have to thank some of the folks from #Authors on the Undernet, whom I've dedicated this work to, because without them I never would have come up with the Institute or the universe it exists in.

A great deal of additional thanks goes to Jennifer Willard, who read the draft before it was finished, Michael van Hese and Erik Fry, who put up with random walls of text on AIM, Greg Borenstein, who was the first one to read the finished version of the draft and caught several errors I'd missed, and my circle of friends on the dreaded Facebook for weighing in with their thoughts on the project and the name of the universe itself.

To all of my friends I haven't mentioned by name, thank you. You're my village, my community, and everything I create is something that you deserve a little bit of credit for, too.

ON WRITING THE PROJECT

What Angels Fear is a project that came about in the most random way. Sitting at my desk one summer afternoon in 2010, while watching *Haven* on Hulu I was struck with the opening for a story. I pulled out a sheaf of notebook paper and a green, felt-tipped pen and started to scribble.

Fourteen pages later, I finally started to figure out what it was I was writing about. Ridley Thys was a side character in a "chain" story begun back in the late 1990's by a group of authors, young and old, from the #Authors chats on the Undernet. In 2003, I got permission from my fellow writers to take the characters we'd played with in that project (which was short-lived to say the least) for a project entitled *When All's Said and Done*, which became my first NaNoWriMo (www.nanowrimo.org) project. Ridley was never mentioned in the project, nor was Laren (Addy), but Kyle, Matthew, and Damon all appeared — as well as Allyson, the unnamed figure that warned Julia to get back to town. At the time I began writing *What Angels Fear*, the "Institute" universe projects had lain dormant for several years, including *When All's Said and Done* (then set in 2004) and its sequel, *When the Gods Cry* (which was set in 2012).

This was much to the chagrin of Jennifer Willard, who had always counted my Institute stories as among her favorites. When I first began to develop the "Institute" universe, she was the person I bounced ideas off of and got to read every word almost as soon as it was written. Much of the credit for my finishing the first draft of *When All's Said and Done* and my eventual return to the universe and the project lies with her.

She was understandably excided when I told her about *What Angels Fear*. However, the work on *What Angels Fear* proved to be a problem, since it shifted the entire trajectory Kyle's story in *When All's Said and Done* and turned what should have been a few editing sweeps into a major redrafting project. It meant that the story took place at a much different time (*What Angels Fear* and *When All's Said and Done* are set in 2009 rather than 2004) and events will play out much, much differently than they did in the original draft. The core of the story, however, will remain the same: victims' fight for justice against those who have wronged them, a desperate soul's mission to save her lover, and the struggle of the Institute's lost "angels" to stop the machinations of the cult that brought them together.

Some people will wonder about my motivations when I wrote *What Angels Fear* and the other works in the "Institute" universe. I realize that I have chosen dangerous ground to tread upon, especially where the Institute's motivations are concerned. I have tried to be even-handed in my approach to religion in this work, which is at its heart a work of paranormal fiction, exclusive of any major hidden agenda. If I have offended some readers, I am deeply sorry. It was not my intention in the least and I hope that you will give me another chance with other works in the future.

Questions and comments, as always, are welcome and can be directed to me via e-mail or my blog at embklitzke.com. I'll be happy to respond.

Thanks for reading!

About the Author

Erin Klitzke has been writing since she was an adolescent, though most of her early works will *never* see the light of day. She got her Bachelor of Arts in history and anthropology from Grand Valley State University and her Master of Arts in history from Oakland University. Much to her mother's occasional dismay, what she does with those degrees is write fiction.

She lives in the northern suburbs of Detroit and enjoys reading, sewing, gaming, and renaissance festivals when she's not creating her own worlds. You can find her on the web at www.embklitzke.com, e-mail her at doc@embklitzke.com, and follow her on Twitter at @EMBKDoc.

Don't miss this exclusive preview of Awakenings: Book One available wherever ebooks are sold and coming soon to print!

Special Preview:

Awakenings
Book One

Erin M. Klitzke

PROLOGUE — DAY ZERO
Marin

I had the music turned up that afternoon, loud enough to drown out the awful muszak that corporate seemed to think was the right kind of music for the store. Cleaning the storage closet wouldn't ordinarily be my idea of fun—it's not really anyone's idea of fun—but it was just one last shift before I started the process of moving to the east coast, to start my graduate work out there. Better yet, it was one last shift that I didn't have to deal with sweaty, demanding customers who wanted everything practically for free.

I wouldn't have been there at all that day unless my sales manager hadn't practically begged for me to come in and do it. Never really could say no to that woman. In the end, I suppose it was best that I was there. I shudder to think what might have happened if I hadn't been, how things would have turned out if I hadn't been there.

If I'm honest with myself, I have to admit I probably wouldn't have survived.

Belting out lyrics to a song I'd heard a dozen times in the last week at the top of my lungs, I was stacking toilet paper on the shelves of the storage closet when I realized I wasn't singing along with the song anymore—I was singing along with static.

"Damn it anyway," I muttered, putting down the last couple rolls on the shelf haphazardly and climbing down from the ladder. *Of course it would flake out when I'm up a ladder. Bloody radio.* The thing was probably older than I was—or at the very least was half my age. It would start to get static-y often enough, though generally not the full on static I was getting right now. I started to fiddle with the tuning dial, leaning against the shelves inside the small space, chewing my lower lip. *I don't remember them saying that the fragments from that asteroid were going to screw with radio signals — satellite, yeah, but radio?* I mumbled a few more curse words as I continued to play with the tuner — static across the board. "Damn it."

The world exploded.

Take a breath and wait to die.
Take a breath and wait to die.
Take a breath and wait to die.
Take a breath —
No.

I coughed hard, trying to roll onto my side, hacking, struggling to breathe. I hadn't had visions in four years. No dreams that I could remember. Only little things. That was all — little, inconsequential things. Nothing like that October day four years ago, when I was so sure that what I saw was real. My ribs hurt, my head rang, and I could still hear those selfsame whispers that I'd heard before as I stood, staring transfixed at what I believed was a mushroom cloud rising just beyond the carillon tower at the university, out in the distance, somewhere across the lake.

Take a breath and wait to die.

No! I hacked and spat, struggling onto my side. The shelves had fallen onto me. All I could hear, now that the voice was gone, was the sound of blood pounding in my ears. No muszak. No nothing.

"Molly! Terra? Anyone?" I continued to try to struggling out from under the shelves, growling in frustration, wincing as I did. *My bruises are going to have bruises. Should get hazard pay for this shit.* "Ungh. Guys! I need help back here."

No one came.

I'm not sure how long it took me to get the shelves off of myself — it took me longer to catch my breath afterwards, stumble to my feet, and force the door open. Longer still for my head to clear as I found myself staring at a red sky, a dark streak trailing from somewhere off in the distance. My eyes stung, tearing—probably from the dust, or from the chemicals that were probably leaking from the bottles I hadn't gotten up on the shelves yet. I tried not to think about those as I stumbled clear of the now open door, blinking blearily.

What the hell just happened? I rubbed at my head. Was I dreaming? Hallucinating? I leaned against the doorframe until I felt it starting to waver under my weight. I stumbled forward in enough time to turn, watch the walls that had sheltered me collapse in on themselves.

"Damn," I mumbled, scrubbing my hand over my face, frowning at the bright red streak of blood across it as I pulled it away. I explored with my fingers, finally finding a gash the length of my pinkie finger along my hairline.

Better deal with that. I stumbled through the wreckage that had once been my store, struggling to come to terms with what had just happened—struggling to sort out what had just happened. I stared up at the sky, watching a few meteorites streaking through the red, leaving bright trails in the sky. Something rumbled in the distance; maybe one of the fragments making landfall. Smoke billowed in the distance, almost in the shape of a mushroom rising lazily against the horizon. My stomach twisted, bucked inside of me.

Like the visions. Like what I saw. Oh god. I sank to my knees, feeling sick, stomach rebelling. *Oh god. Oh god…*

Take a breath and wait to die.

"Ungh. What hit me?"

"I think that it was a bookshelf, but I could be wrong." Muscles straining, Carolyn and Jacqueline heaved the metal shelves, now bereft of books, off of Davon. The books from those library shelves lay scattered all around the tow-headed man, who lay sprawled on the library floor, looking slightly dazed but otherwise all right. Jacqueline offered him her arm and he took it, pulling himself to his feet and cracking his neck. Four of them had come up to the stacks that morning, only to have the world seem to explode half an hour into their sojourn. Jacqueline couldn't even remember why they'd come up here, now. She was just grateful they all seemed to be in one piece.

Nearby, Rory was picking his way through the wreckage toward the doorway to the stairwell, which stood ajar, a yawning maw looking into a stairwell choked with drifting dust. The building wasn't creaking, nor was there the sound of the masonry starting to crack. Maybe that was a good sign. Maybe.

It should be a good sign, right? Jacqueline started to pick her way down the row of what had once been the stacks, toward Rory and their way down and out of the building. Goosebumps rose along her bare arms. She wanted out of the building, suddenly silent and eerie as a tomb.

"How do the stairs look, Rory?"

"Uhm. Okay, I think. Give me a second." He jerked the door a bit further open, casting a baleful glance toward Jacqueline. "This is the last time you're ever getting me into a library. *Ever.*"

She tried to laugh, but it sounded like a bitter croak. Rory hated libraries, feared them. He'd always said they gave him a bad feeling, made his skin crawl, made him feel like someone was watching him. Marin usually just laughed at him and said he'd probably spent too much time in one in a past life, which usually earned her a dirty look. Jacqueline wasn't sure what to think about that—then or now.

Carolyn shook her head, looking bewildered, only half visible in the dim and the drifting dust. "What was that, really?"

"I don't know." Jacqueline looked back toward the door to the stairwell, illuminated from the skylight above. Rory had pushed the door most of the way open and was standing near the top step of the stairway leading down, on the solid stone and steel landing.

"Looks okay from here," he called back to the rest. He started down, slowly at first, then a little more quickly as it became clear that the stairwell was, in fact, stable. Eager to escape as ever. Jacqueline couldn't blame him. She had to admit the idea of being entombed in a giant concrete box wasn't a very appealing prospect.

Davon shook his head. "Guess there's a reason it won design awards in the '70s."

Carolyn shook her head, looking as grim as Jacqueline felt. The three started to slowly make their way down the stairs after Rory, down the single flight to the library's main level.

It would have been pitch black but for the windows—most of them broken, now—along the outer walls. Dust drifted lazily in the air. The banks of computers were dark. No one was within sight.

"Guys?" A voice called from the far side of the circulation desk. Kellin peeked over the edge of it, her gray eyes wide. She must have heard their footsteps in the strange silence that blanketed the world. Her voice was almost shaky. "I think something really bad just happened."

"You think?" Rory's voice dripped with his usual sarcasm, but even that seemed strained. Jacqueline winced.

Something bad really did *just happen.* She cleared her throat, picking her way toward Kellin. "Were you the only one working circ desk today, Kel?"

Kellin nodded, raking lank tangles of brown curls out of her face as she straightened and climbed over the desk with Jacqueline's help. "Drew was down in archives, I think, though, in the basement."

"...not anymore." The tall man looked about as tired as any of them had ever seen him. A bruise was forming on his cheekbone and one arm hung a little more limply than it should have. "Wrenched my shoulder pushing a fiche reader out from in front of the door," he explained, slowly working the arm up and around in a circle. It popped sickeningly and he winced, then worked it around in an arc again—no sound the second time around. "Any of you see what happened?"

"Just a flash. Boom. Windows blown out." Kellin frowned.

"Two flashes." Davon rubbed his head. "I saw two. Was looking at the corner window on the second floor."

"Sky's red," Rory muttered from near the shattered windows. "Come see."

The friends crowded close, peering through the shattered window, craning their necks toward the sky. Clouds drifted lazily through the air, but not against blue. The sky was indeed red, deep and angry, streaked dark somewhere high above the normal summer clouds.

"It looks like blood," Rory mumbled, staring at it. Jacqueline made the sign of the cross on herself, pressing a hand against the silver and gold crucifix she wore around her neck, a gift from her long-ago first communion.

Her heart fluttered. *Is this the end of the world?*

Kellin looked sidelong at her, brow furrowing slightly, and said softly, "No. It's the beginning."

o   o   o

Half an hour later, they had taken stock of the situation—and found it wasn't good. Standing in the middle of the plaza, they surveyed the wreck of what had once been their university campus. Several of the old, stoutly-built cinderblock, concrete, and glass buildings on the central plaza were already half ruined. All the glass in Au Sable Hall's atrium was shattered, glittering greenish on the ground. They'd collectively decided that it probably wouldn't be best to necessarily trust the structural integrity of the rest of the buildings around them—especially in the light of what they continued to watch.

Meteorites continued to lazily rain from the sky, one or two every five or ten minutes. It was hard to tell where they were landing, how far away they were landing. A few times, they could see fire licking into the sky in the distance or feel the earth tremble beneath their feet. They'd seen no sign of other survivors, but they hadn't expected there to be many people on campus, anyhow—it was a Sunday morning, after all, in the middle of August. Semesters had ended. Most people were back home, enjoying their last few days of freedom before the new term began. Just a few days before, they'd been discussing how empty the university grounds were in these waning days of summer, before move-ins started for the fall semester but after the end of the summer term.

Matthew Astoris had struggled up one steep side of the ravine about twenty minutes after the six had emerged from the library, one of the few relatively intact buildings on this section of the campus. He was tired, and gratefully accepted a bottle of water the friends had looted from one of the broken vending machines in the library's lobby.

"Something must've come down downstream of here," he reported after he'd gotten about half the bottle into him, slumped against the concrete steps up to the library's doors. "River's moving faster than it should be."

Davon grimaced at hearing that. Drew just shook his

head. "Nothing we can do about that," he said quietly, looking around. "Your phone working, Matt?"

Matt shook his head. "Can't get a signal. Can you?"

"Nothing. None of us can get anything." He blew out a breath through his teeth, looking around. A few people were stumbling up from underneath Lake Michigan Hall, they could see at the end of the plaza. Tala was waving.

"Guess they were down in the cave," Davon muttered, shaking his head. The slang for the anthropology lab in the basement of Lake Michigan Hall was one they'd all become accustomed to hearing.

"Guess so," Jacqueline echoed. She glanced at Rory, Drew, and Kellin—the trio had withdrawn a little from the rest, each looking at each other with strange expressions on their faces—guilt, was it? No, not guilt. Something else. Reluctance, almost. "What's wrong?"

Drew winced. "Don't worry about it. Look, we're going to go take a look at Little Mac and stuff…why don't you guys take Matt's bag and go grab whatever food and water and stuff you can out of those broken vending machines? Might need them before this is over."

"All right. Come back for the rest of us before you go take a look beyond Commons, huh?"

"We will," he assured her. She nodded, watching the trio head down the plaza toward the pedestrian bridge over the ravine. Chewing the inside of her lip, she slowly turned back toward the library, mounting the steps.

"I'm getting the impression that this might be a little bigger than a local thing," Carolyn said quietly.

"I wish I could say I felt like they were wrong," Jacqueline muttered back.

"…damn. I was hoping you didn't feel that way, too."

Jacqueline shook her head slowly. "World feels different, Care. Don't ask me how, but it does."

"You bet it does." Carolyn shouldered the door open, holding it ajar for Jacqueline. Matt and Davon remained on the steps, waiting for Tala and her fellow shovel-bums to make it across the plaza to them. "Nice to know I'm not the only one who suddenly feels that way."

"I don't like it."

"Neither do I," she sighed. "But something else tells me we don't get a vote about it."

Jacqueline frowned, grabbing a few plastic bags from behind the circulation desk, the kind usually used for books. She handed one to Carolyn and began to gather up the bottles of water and juice that had spilled from the broken machine as Carolyn started gathering the food from the other machine up. "Would you really want one?"

"Good question." Carolyn paused a moment, frowning. "I don't think I would."

"I didn't think so, either."

"So what are we going to do?"

"Not sure." Jacqueline paused, too, staring at her friend. "Muddle through somehow?"

"Business as usual."

"As usual as it can get under the circumstances, I guess." She resumed stuffing bottled water into her bag, trying to will her stomach to settle down. She felt sick. "...what do you think is going to happen to us?"

"I'm trying not to think about that just yet," Carolyn admitted, starting to help her with the bottles. "Right now, I'm just trusting Drew and Kellin. And Matthew. They'll figure something out. Some kind of solution for at least the short term."

"And the long term?"

"That's what I'm trying not to think about." Carolyn blew a breath out through her teeth. "We don't even really know what happened out there, Jac. Shouldn't get *too* ahead of ourselves, right?"

The ground shuddered beneath them, more violently than all the previous tremors. Jacqueline muttered an oath under her breath and pushed to her feet; Carolyn was already headed for the door.

"What the hell is that?"

"I don't know."

The ground was still moving beneath them as they scrambled outside.

"What's going on?" Kellin, Drew, and Rory were making a mad dash back toward the knot of survivors gathering outside of the library.

Matthew looked grim. "Earthquake," he said calmly. "Meteorites probably hit something and caused it." The ground gradually stopped shaking. The geology student slowly stood up, squinting at the sky. "I think they were wrong," he said quietly, watching as another meteorite streaked through the sky distantly, disappearing behind the tree line. "These aren't negligible at all."

"You're saying this is from the asteroid they blew up? The one that everyone threw missiles at so it wouldn't do something like this."

It didn't matter who the voice came from; Matthew answered all the same, voice grim. "I don't think they exactly knew what they were dealing with, or the consequences that could result from the actions they took. This...I don't think they expected this at all." He picked up his bag. "We need to rig up some shelters and get as much food together as we can. Hopefully, this is isolated and the National Guard will show up soon enough to help us sort out this mess."

The National Guard isn't going to be able to fix what's just gone wrong with this world. Jacqueline tried to kill the thought before it manifested, but failed. When had she become such a pessimist? A glance toward the bloody sky answered that question quickly enough—apparently, in the moment of a flash of light when the world went dark.

o   o   o

I don't like this at all. Kellin frowned darkly to herself, standing near the rim of the ravine—a few feet back, in case the ground decided to move again, as it had a few times since they'd come out of the library and onto the plaza. She stared down at the ravine, at the creek. Something had stirred in the last hour, and was still stirring now.

Three dozen of them—no, forty of them now. Survivors from the campus. Eight had already left despite urgings to stay put. Kellin already knew they'd never see those eight again. She could feel it. It wasn't a good feeling, either, especially because she knew they wouldn't be the last to slip away, never to be seen again.

There was safety in numbers and safety *here*, even though no one quite believed it.

She exhaled through her teeth, watching the not-quite-imaginary ripples down near the creek that ran along the bottom of the ravine. They quavered and swirled, twisting back on each other, more than she was used to seeing them do. They wove themselves into knots that she could feel tightening, the lines suddenly changing, the fabric warping.

She glanced toward Drew. "You can feel it, too, can't you?"

The tall man grimaced, following her gaze. "For the first time, I can *see* it," he murmured. He'd never been able to see these things before, only in snatches and snippets, fleeting glimpses, but he'd always been able to feel it. He looked at her for a moment. "What do we *do*, Kellin? You understand this more than the rest of us."

She snorted softly. "Rory understands, too. His understanding is just *unique*." She crouched, hugging her knees and staring down. The ground trembled a moment, then stilled. "It's bad, Drew," she mumbled. "The whole…everything's destabilizing. The lines…"

"Shifting erratically."

She nodded. "And faster than they should. Something hitting the river itself shouldn't do this, either, not like this. Destabilize it, yes, but it doesn't just feel like it's the lines through here. It feels like the entire fabric is being twisted."

"And torn."

"And torn," she echoed, swallowing. *And the others can't grasp this yet. Some of them will soon, but not yet. But they'll ask. They'll ask me, as if I have the answers to all of their questions. What do I tell them?* She exhaled quietly. "It's not good."

"But it's...it's the beginning, you said?"

Kellin blinked. *I didn't think he heard me say it.* She licked her lips almost nervously. The words had slipped out when she had felt Jacqueline's question, thought so strongly that it was audible to anyone even remotely sensitive. It *was* a beginning, though Kellin herself wasn't sure of what—but something different. A new world, maybe? A new age? Probably. She shook her head slightly. "Of something. Not an end. Well. An end and a beginning at the same time. Something different. Everything's changing. I'm not really sure that it's...well. That it's an awful thing."

"Hope you're right," Drew mumbled, staring at the tortured lines below that he could feel but couldn't see.

"So do I." She smiled ruefully, watching the rippling and swirling below. "Has anyone found Marin yet?" *Marin will be able to help. She can help me figure out what to say. How to explain it all, when they ask us. She's good at that.*

Silence met her question. She started to feel a little queasy and looked up at Drew quizzically. He was frowning. Her brow furrowed.

"What is it?"

"Marin went to work. Got called in last-minute." Drew scratched his head. "Not sure if she was off yet when this started."

Damn. Kellin swallowed rising bile. *Damn and damn! If she didn't—if she's dead—I don't know what I'm going to do.* "Hope she made it back."

"I'm sure Matt does, too."

Kellin winced. "Yeah." Matthew was Marin's younger brother, less than two years younger than his sister. They'd been raised by their aunt after their parents had died while they were in high school; cancer took her two years before. Marin was all he had left these days, especially after he'd transferred to the university a year ago after breaking up with his fiancé. That had been for the best, Marin had said repeatedly in the wake of the incident. She was probably right, though Matthew had been slow to recover, to try to make new friends to replace those he'd lost.

Kellin crouched and drew in the dust with a fingertip near her feet. "If this is what it might be…we need her, Drew."

"Preaching to the choir, Kellin. I realize we'll need her." He glanced back over his shoulder. Rory was on his way toward them from the knot of people, which seemed to have decreased by a couple more bodies. More were leaving, too scared to stay. "This is going to be long-term."

"Choir." Kellin sighed. "You and I—and Rory, too, I think—know it's going to be long-term. This isn't isolated. Have *you* seen the meteorites stop coming down? I haven't. Sky looks like it's getting worse." She didn't mention the strange wind, or the dark clouds they'd been watching rising in the west. She didn't *need* to mention the continuing ground tremors, or the feeling of the very fabric of the world, of its power-lines, twisting back on itself, unraveling.

"We drew the short straw," Rory announced as he joined them. He grinned at Kellin's quizzical look. "They want us to hike out to M-45, see what we can see. Count cars in the parking lots on that end of campus." The grin faded. "Figure out how many people we should be looking for. How many bodies we might be finding before this is over."

Kellin winced. *Of course there'll be dead. I just…wish there wouldn't be.* She slowly straightened, crouching again as a ground tremor stole her balance momentarily. The sound of breaking glass echoed off the trees and the ruined buildings. *Not good. These buildings aren't designed for seismic stability.*

She made it all the way upright on the second try. Chewing on the inside of her lip, she chafed her hands over bare arms. "Someone else checking the dorms?"

"Tala volunteered. She and some of the other anthro students, plus Leah and Jacqueline." Leah Vandenberg was in the nursing program—Jacqueline had met her in one of their freshman chemistry classes and they'd been friends since. Rory frowned at her. "Are you cold, Kel?"

She grimaced. "A little. Wind's chilly."

"It is," Drew admitted, eying Rory.

Rory just shrugged. "Could be this is making the weather turn?"

"Pray it doesn't," Kellin mumbled. "If it does, things are going to get very messy very quickly, I think."

"We'll find a way to make it work." The optimism in Rory's voice was unusual, to say the least. Normally, the criminal justice student was the most pessimistic of the bunch—something in the midst of this insanity must have put him in a good mood.

The bleaker the straits, the more perky he gets, I guess. Maybe it's the challenge. Or adrenaline. Kellin sighed again. *I hope I don't hate what we're going to see when he finally comes down from this high.* "Right. I'm thinking we'd probably be better off going the long way around rather than trying Little Mac. Let's go."

The wind was worse out in the open, away from the sheltering trees of the ravines, whistling between buildings, down along the brickwork pathways of the campus. The clocktower was listing sideways. Kellin grimaced.

"…that's probably not good, huh?"

Rory followed her gaze and shook his head, pursing his lips half thoughtfully. "Nope. Nope, probably not good at all. Think we need to avoid this section until it comes down."

Kellin nodded. Drew nudged her. "Let's keep moving."

Together, the trio forged onward, moving quickly along the pathways of campus, skirting wide of buildings along the campus's main drag rather than moving along the ravine's edge. They were checking the parking lots, after all, to do a count of how many people should be around.

The field house was mostly a pile of wreckage and rubble, twisted metal and shattered glass, but the parking lots around it were mercifully empty, it appeared, which made Kellin exhale a sigh of relief. *Gods, but I hope there's not many. I hope there's not many. Please let there not be many.* She wasn't looking forward to burying anyone, though she already knew they were going to—and probably many—in the hours and days and weeks to come.

In the years to come.

They continued along the concrete sidewalk, stopping as the ground began to heave. The trio grasped for each other, hanging on for balance. Kellin went down, and Drew took a knee to steady Rory before he joined Kellin on the ground.

The feeling of ley lines twisting made her stomach flip-flop, and for a moment she thought she was going to offer everything she'd eaten that day up to the grass nearby. Kellin swallowed hard, covering her eyes with her hand, trying to breathe through her nose so she wouldn't vomit.

Drew squeezed her shoulder. His face was pinched, pale—clearly he was having the same problems. A glance at Rory revealed that while he struggled to keep a straight face, he was suffering from the same wrenching feelings as they were.

"This is bad," Kellin whispered.

Rory nodded grimly. If he was feeling it with the same intensity as they, it was *very* bad. For all sides, and all stripes. As the tremors eased, he reached down, pulling Kellin to her feet and steadying her gently. "Come on. Sooner we get all this done, sooner we can get back to the others and give *them* a hand." He glanced toward Mackinac Hall, one of the largest buildings on campus, and grimaced, pointing. "Look. Part of the south corner's come down."

"Columns in the courtyard are probably down, too," Drew murmured.

Kellin nodded. "We knew that this section was probably

the most solid but not," she mumbled, scrubbing a hand over her eyes. *Something destabilizing below. Pilings can't fix that. They weren't building these things to be seismically sound, anyhow. Why worry about that crap this far away from a major fault line? Something devastating would have to happen for us to get quakes here.*

Something like this. She exhaled shakily. "Let's go, guys. You're right. We need to get this done so we can move on to the next thing. Whatever that's going to be."

Drew grunted. They moved on, heading toward the resident parking lots on the so-called "freshman" end of campus. Several of the dorms were already collapsed — Niemeyer looked like something had crashed into it, Frey was rubble, Stafford collapsed as well, and the buildings nearest to the tree line were simply *gone*, buried as rubble and under fallen trees. A few scattered cars were in the parking lots nearest to the dorms — some of them belonged to the friends and were checked off a mental list each of the three were keeping of approximately how many people might still be yet to be found on the campus — alive or otherwise.

There was one car, an old silver BMW, settled in a corner parking spot not far from where they were standing. Kellin stared at it for a few long moments. It was naggingly familiar, though she couldn't quite place it. Her frown grew as she wrestled with her own mind, pushing the impressions she was catching from the ravines, from the world around her, of twisting leylines and shifting energies, to the back of her mind as she tried to remember.

Finally, it clicked. "...that's Thom's car." *Why is Thom's car still here? He was driving to Chicago this weekend to see his folks. And he's got that interview Monday for that job down there. Why the hell would his car still be here?* "Did he take the train down from Holland to the city, Drew?"

Drew looked at her, blinking. "Who?"

"Thom! His car's still here. Did you drive him to the station?"

"Thom didn't go to Chicago this weekend."

Why wouldn't he go? That interview...he made it sound like his big shot at being someone and something. "What about his interview? Seeing his parents?"

Drew shrugged a little. "He called them Thursday night and said that he had something come up, had to reschedule. I don't know how the rest of that conversation went. He seemed a little out of sorts." He scratched the back of his head. "When I asked him, though, he said that Chicago wasn't going anywhere, and neither were his parents. He didn't want to miss Marin leaving."

Rory glanced back at them. "Wasn't that why he was going to go to the city this weekend and stay 'til Tuesday in the first place? Because he *didn't* want to be around for that?"

Drew shrugged again. "Guess he couldn't bring himself to miss saying goodbye. Even to Marin."

Especially to Marin. Kellin grimaced. "We have to find him if he's still here."

"With any luck, he'll find us. He usually does." Rory hopped down off the curb. "Come on. More lots to check. Should check Kleiner while we're here. See if there's anyone there."

"What if there is and they're dead?" Kellin tried to catch the words as they slipped out of her mouth, to no avail. Her tongue had gotten away from her — again.

Rory stopped, turning toward her slowly. He exhaled, then shrugged slightly. "Then I guess we bury them."

"Was afraid you'd say that."

The façade cracked and he grimaced. "Better than leaving them to rot, Kel. Come on. Let's get this over with."

Two — Day Zero
Marin

Another stumbling step drew me closer to my destination. The sky grew dark slowly, though whether with gathering night or something else, I wasn't certain. I doubted the former and suspected the latter, in the moments I was truly aware, truly lucid.

My head was still ringing, pounding, and my body ached. My feet had never really hurt quite so much as they did at that very moment. I wasn't even sure how long I'd been walking anymore, either, just stumbled slowly on my way down what was left of a highway, from where I worked toward where I lived, on autopilot, knowing—just knowing—that I had to get back somehow.

I daydreamed as I struggled along, letting currents of memory and imaginings carry me at least temporarily away from my body, from the aches and the trembling, the tremors of the ground and the sick feeling in my stomach that came with them, feelings that grew with every painful step I took along the way.

An exhaled breath sounded like my name. I rolled slowly, rotating in the cocoon of his arms, nuzzling his jaw lightly as I opened my eyes lazily to stare at him. His eyes were half-lidded and he smiled sleepily at me, reaching up and brushing hair away from my face.

"Almost afraid to get used to this."

The corner of my mouth curled in a smile. "Why's that?"

"Well, for one thing, it's the first time you've actually not been distracted when we've done this." He laced his fingers through my hair and drew my face down to his, kissing my forehead gently, tongue sampling the sweat wrought by previous exertions. "First time you haven't said we're being watched, or something equally weird."

I stiffened, restraining myself. Something was watching us, but I'd elected not to say so. Elected not to once again end this before it started, to not 'kill the mood' as I'd managed to before. It wasn't fair to either us – but what was more unfair was the fact that he denied feeling the same things that I was. I knew he could feel things, could see them. But for the past six months, he'd done nothing but deny that. It had put a strain on us – on us as a couple, as a thing. The fact that he kept calling it weird, though, and denying what we both knew…that was starting to put a strain on me. I cared about him too much to let him blind himself to what he was really sensing – what we were sensing, and feeling.

He felt me tense and sighed, letting go and sagging against the mattress, looking away. "Damn it anyway, Marin."

I sighed, pushing myself upright. "I'll go."

"It's your place."

I shrugged, padding across the floor to find my clothes, lost somewhere between the door and the bed. "I'll take a walk. You can do whatever. I really…yeah. I'm tired of fighting you on all of this, Thom."

"I can't live with the delusions."

"They're not and you know it, unless we're both crazy." *I yanked my pants on, followed by my shirt. He didn't say anything in response. I turned toward him, nodding firmly.* "I'll be back in an hour, Thom."

He didn't say anything as I walked out the door.

"Ungh." My knees were scraped as I picked myself up off the ground again, peering blearily down the highway. Landmarks looked familiar. I knew where I was—I'd stumbled at least another few miles since the last time I was aware of where I was. I rubbed at my eyes, trying to ignore the pounding in my head and the grittiness around my eyes. God, it hurt. It hurt so much. I stumbled another few steps before stopping, blinking as my head cleared a little.

That's the Grand River. But the bridge…god. The bridge…

I rubbed my eyes again, making sure I was seeing what I was seeing.

The M-45 bridge over the Grand River had collapsed. Bits of the bridge had already begun to drift downriver, moving quickly — more quickly than the Grand should. One car was overturned on the bank, half-sunk into the mud. I shuddered and stumbled sideways, retching onto the shoulder of the road. The air stank of death already. How long had it been since it all started?

The church to my left, the one near the riverfront, had been obliterated by something. The parking lot was packed. I shuddered again. That's where the smell was coming from. I prayed that was the *only* place it was coming from.

I spat twice after puking, then pushed myself upright again, trying to study the bridge critically, figure out a safe way across the broken concrete to the other side. My head swam as I struggled to make sense of a path across, failing miserably. I pressed the heel of my hand against my temple, willing myself to focus, if only for a few minutes, just so I could make it across, get closer to *home*.

I stumbled onward, picking my way across the broken concrete carefully. I lost a shoe somewhere along the way, climbing across the broken pieces, stumbling up and down the pitched slabs. I dimly could hear someone calling my name as I made my way slowly, agonizingly across, but I couldn't spare the brainpower or the energy in trying to figure out who was calling me — or if it was even real.

I lost my footing on a particularly steep bit, slid down the slab, scraping my legs up something fierce. I groaned, lacking even the energy to get back up again.

It seems stable enough. Maybe I can just rest here for a few minutes.

"Marin!"

I looked up, squinting. "Rory?"

He turned away. "She's down here!" He eased down over the edge of the slab, sliding down toward me, getting a shoulder under me. "You're alive."

"What're you doing here?" I gasped as a stab of pain shot

up my leg as I tried to straighten up with his help. I glared down toward my foot, feeling betrayed. Had I stepped on something?

"We came to see what M-45 looked like. Good thing we did, huh?" He heaved me upright despite my protesting muscles. Drew appeared at the top of the slab and reached an arm down. Rory heaved me up toward him and somehow I caught Drew's arm. Between the two of them, they got me up onto more stable ground beyond the midpoint. They practically carried me to the other side of the river.

"The Baptist church over there..."

Kellin was at the end of the bridge, waiting for us. "We know. It's not much better on campus, honestly, but we'll see. Not sure how many are dead yet. I think lots."

I had to nod, shivering. "I think so, too, Kel." The ground quaked again. I shuddered and found myself unable to stop. I was so cold...

"She's in shock," Rory mumbled. Drew picked me up, cradling me like a child.

"We'll take care of it."

I wanted to ask how, but I didn't have time before I just sagged into darkness.

o   o   o

"Ungh." My limbs felt like jelly and my feet were on fire. I wasn't sure how long I'd been out; all I knew was that whatever I was on was mostly soft, there was a pillow, and I was still utterly exhausted. I sagged, groaning weakly again and scrubbing a hand over my face. Never before had I felt like utter crap, and in that moment I prayed I'd never experience such a feeling ever again.

"Marin?"

I groaned, rolling onto my side and making an attempt to force myself up into a sitting position. It took a minute and a lot of effort, but I managed to get myself upright. "What happened?"

"You passed out, that's what happened."

I feel like I should've stayed unconscious. "Thanks for stating the obvious, Carolyn. What's going on?"

"Pretty sure the world ended about six hours ago." She moved over, sat down with me on the mattress they'd clearly salvaged from the dorms. "Did you walk that whole way up here from the mall?"

Did I? God. I must have. I rubbed at my eyes. "I must have. My legs hurt."

"You've got a knot on your head the size of a baseball," she told me, grimacing. "And I totally can't blame you if your legs hurt. Mine would definitely hurt."

I smiled weakly at her, drawing one leg painfully up against my chest, stretching my thigh muscles gently. "Everyone okay?"

She frowned. "Depends on what you mean by everyone. I was in the library with Jacqueline and Davon and Rory. I've seen some of the others. Don't know exactly how many are still alive out here. Hopefully more than I'm afraid of."

"Hopefully," I echoed. "Do you guys have any ideas?"

"Forty, maybe? I'm not sure. I've been sitting with you since Jacqueline and Leah decided you'd live, waiting for you to wake up. They told me I was probably better off here than...well...elsewhere, doing something else."

Probably right. Carolyn doesn't need to see half of what she might be seeing in the near future here. I suppressed a shudder, remembering the stench of the church. *Definitely doesn't...sooner or later, though, we won't be able to keep it from her anymore.* I leaned into her shoulder, closing my eyes again and sighing tiredly. "Have they checked everywhere?"

"Not sure, really." Carolyn reached down, picked up the blanket that had been spread over me and wrapped it around my shoulders. I gave her a questioning glance, but she just shook her head. "You're shaking, Marin."

"I'm tired. That's all." I tugged the blanket closer. It felt cooler than it should have been — much cooler. I squinted toward the sky. Sullen red, streaked in dark gray. *I don't like the look of that.* I took a deep breath, exhaling slowly.

Take a breath and wait to die.

I squeezed my eyes shut.

"Marin?"

"I'm okay." I started to try to push to my feet, gasping at the pain in my calves and ankles. "Ungh. Ow." I sat back down abruptly, blinking stinging tears from my eyes. *God, that* hurts.

She looked at me quizzically. "Who do you need?"

"Not sure. Who took charge?"

Carolyn blushed a bit. "I'm not really sure, honestly."

Wonderful. I sank back down, waited a long moment for the pain to abate slightly before asking, "Where are we, exactly?" *That she'll know.*

"Hills outside of Copeland and Robinson." Carolyn hugged her knee against her chest, flipping dark hair over her shoulder. "They looked like the most stable areas to set up shop."

I nodded tiredly. *Makes sense. More solid ground than anywhere else on campus. Dorms would fall back down into the ravine before they fall forward onto the hills, if they survived the initial...whatever that was.* A glance outside confirmed that they *had* survived, but I could already see the nasty crack forming in the end wall of Copeland. They wouldn't last. "Mattress come from inside?"

"Yeah. Some of the camps staff is hauling crap down and out. We're not sure how stable the buildings are. Davon's been checking, I guess. Outer shells on some of them are probably okay, it's everything else we're worried about, maybe. I'm not sure. Like I said, they told me to stay with you." Carolyn grimaced. "Glad it's them in there and not me. Getting out of the library was bad enough."

Of course it's still standing. "Was it bad in there?"

She shrugged, pushing to her feet and moving over to a

bag that lay beneath the shade of our makeshift shelter—shelter built, I realized, from stacked and pinned furniture from the dorms shoved up against one of the trees on this particular hill. From the bag, she produced a bottle of water and a package of crackers. I threw her a questioning glance and she smiled guiltily. "We sort of raided the C-store," she told me, pressing the crackers into my hand. "Rory said Jacqueline and I shouldn't freak out too much."

I couldn't help myself. "And you listened?" I unwrapped the crackers.

She shrugged. "It's not looting if everyone else is dead, right?"

I stopped, almost choking on the cracker I'd just shoved into my mouth. Carolyn scrambled to uncap the water bottle and thrust it toward me. I gulped some down, coughed a little, then downed some more before I regained the ability to speak—or sputter, as it were. "Did you just...?"

She shrugged again, not making eye contact with me. "We all realize that something's gone terribly, horribly wrong, Marin. It's the end, isn't it?" She finally looked me in the eye. "Like what you used to talk about sometimes with Kellin and Drew and Rory, the stuff you told me I could ignore. The stuff you used to see. That stuff."

My breath caught in my throat and I thought I would just fall over onto the mattress again right then and there. Was she actually saying this? Our Carolyn? *Our* Carolyn? She was the only one we'd tried to shelter more than anyone else. She was the one that we'd agreed maybe couldn't handle the strain of knowing, of learning—and yet, she'd been the *safe* one, even more than Jacqueline or Davon, because she wouldn't ask—Davon just thought we were all crazy, I was fairly certain, and Jacqueline would have started asking questions that we weren't ready to answer. But Davon didn't understand—not yet—and we were going to have to sort out a way to tell Jacqueline without accidentally breaking her. It wouldn't be easy, but they would eventually accept it. They wouldn't deny it. *Not like...* I stopped the thought before it got rolling.

Carolyn grimaced and started to stand up. "I'm going to go find Kellin. She said I should when you woke up."

I held up a hand to forestall her departure. "Carolyn, wait." I scrubbed my hand over my eyes, crackers half forgotten in my lap, bottle of water locked in the other hand. My head was slowly clearing—too slow for my comfort. I took another gulp of water. "How...how do you know?"

She shrugged a little again, sinking down to kneel in front of me. "Just a feeling, I guess. Everything feels like the end of the world, anyway." She frowned, fidgeting a little. "If it wasn't, someone would've made it to us by now, anyway. We'd have seen something." She bit her lip. "I just...I know, Marin. And you know, too. It's all over your face, and Rory's and Kel's and Drew's. You all know it." She rocked up to her feet. "Better walking into whatever comes next with open eyes rather than denying it until I stop breathing." She managed a smile. "Trying to look at it like a big adventure. I can think of worse teams to get stuck on. Drink your water. I'm going to get Kellin."

I nodded mutely, unable to contain my shock. *Our Carolyn indeed. Never saw that coming.* I drank my water, trying to slow down—gulping it wasn't going to do me any good. *Is this how it's going to be? They'll just start...waking up before we've had the time to properly prepare them?* I grimaced. Maybe that was why Kellin had been so insistent on talking to me quickly after I woke up. I suspected it was otherwise, though. She'd have other things to pick my brain about. I'd be the one to bring up the others waking up to the abilities we knew that they must have. *Another Thom isn't going to help anyone in this situation.* I winced, hugging my knee against my chest.

"One was enough," I mumbled to myself. "Davon will probably deny it, too, though. Maybe." I rested my forehead against my knee and sighed. He probably would, at that. At least at first. But maybe he wouldn't. We'd have to see.

There were a lot of things we'd have to see.

"You okay, Marin?"

I rested my chin on my knee, looking up toward Kellin and managing a shrug. "Thinking, mostly. Not good things."

"Not a lot of good to think about right now, 'cept that we're what's left of...well. What's left." She came over and sat down next to me on the mattress. "What's up?"

I grimaced. "Carolyn." She blinked at me, momentarily confused. I sighed and shook my head. "She knows what we know, I think. Sort of. She feels...she feels that something's gone wrong, beyond just saying it. I can tell. It's in her eyes. She *knows*, Kel."

Kellin's voice was quiet. "She does? She...she is? Aware of all of it? Can sense it?"

"Yes," I whispered, exhaling slowly. "I'm pretty sure of it." *For better or for worse, she's aware. I guess we'll know soon enough.*

Kellin didn't say anything for a long moment. "Well," she said finally, "I guess that's a bridge we have to cross sooner than we'd have liked." She scrubbed her hands over her face and leaned back against her palms, looking at me. "We knew that it might eventually happen."

"Eventually. We also decided it might *never* happen in this lifetime, so why worry about it?" I blew out a breath through my teeth. "If *she's* becoming aware, Kellin, what about the others? They can't be far behind." *We always thought she would be the last one to Awaken. Maybe we were wrong. I hope we are. I just want to be able to take this one person at a time. Carolyn first, everyone else later.*

"A bridge we'll cross when we get to it. We've got other issues."

"I'm sure we do," I mumbled. I dug around in my pocket for my keys, coming up empty.

"We took them already. That's how we got into the other dorms."

"Oh." I chewed the inside of my lip. *Of course they'd loot my keys. If furniture is going to equal shelter...* "Who's in charge, Kellin?"

"Right now? We're kind of leading by consensus. Professor Doyle seems like he's in pretty good shape, now that his arm's set." Greg Doyle was maybe eight years older than me — in his early thirties, I thought — and taught biology. I'd only met him a few times, at meetings for the campus pagan group, which I'd helped to create and then promptly abandoned as things got...well...too fuzzy for me. Kellin had stuck it out, probably just to see if she could channel some of the members in positive directions. I wasn't sure how successful she'd been — we didn't talk about the organization much. "Haven't really found anyone else other than you that's even moderately in the realm of authority figure." The only thing that made me an authority figure was that in addition to my off-campus job, I was one of the people in charge of the summer camps staff — which had resulted in me having a lot of keys, mostly to the dormitories and a few associated buildings. Between me and Davon, we probably had keys to most of the campus and knew how to find the rest.

I nodded slowly, taking another long swallow of water. "It's a Sunday. Guess we can't expect much of anyone to actually be on campus, right?"

"For better or worse," Kellin murmured, looking at her hands, which were stained with dirt.

Oh. Oh, Kellin. I reached over, squeezed her arm gently. "How many have you buried already?"

"Thirty or forty, maybe," she said quietly. "Long graves — trenches, really. Out by the PAC." She paused, then looked at me. "We haven't found Thom yet."

Why would they be looking for Thom? Thom left for Chicago...he's not here. He didn't want to stay to say good-bye to me. Interview was too important. All that rot. He's gone. My throat tightened. I didn't want him to be gone, to be dead, but that was probably the reality.

I fought to keep my voice steady. "Thom's in Chicago. We're not going to find him here. He's probably dead, like most of the rest." The words tasted like ash in my mouth. I felt sick just saying the words. *I'm never going to fight with him again because I never* can. *Because he's gone. I'll never see him again. Damn it. What I wouldn't give to fight with him one more time.* I swallowed hard. Now wasn't the time to mourn him — there'd be a chance eventually, but not just yet. Right now, we had to make it through the next few days, the next few weeks. I could come apart later.

"His car's still here, Marin. Drew said he decided not to go."

I stared at her. *When did he decide not to go?* Why *did he decide not to go? That job was so, so important to him. Idiot! Why didn't he...* My chest tightened. *Oh god. That means he's still...that he's...* "So he's here somewhere?"

She nodded. "We have no idea where, though."

I stared at her for a long moment. She looked the same as always, right down to her necklace that wasn't a necklace. *A way to find lost things. One use for scrying, for dowsing. Not just for finding water, but finding anything.* "...then what the hell are you wearing that around your neck for?"

"Huh?" Kellin looked down toward the finger of rose quartz she wore around her neck on a slender silver chain. It was her pendulum, one she wore like a necklace so she'd always have it on hand. She blinked a moment at it, then looked back at me. "What?"

She must have hit her head. "You can scry for lost things, can't you? I've seen you find your keys with that thing before."

Kellin shook her head, hard, as if she was struggling to clear it. "You want me to *dowse* for *Thom*?"

"You said you can't find him." I started pushing to my feet again, grimacing. *Fuck it. Push past. Time enough to rest when you're dead, or when he's dead. Or something. Need to find him first.* I smiled grimly to myself. *So I can slug him, then kiss him, and scream at him for not telling me that he wasn't going to Chicago this weekend.* I wavered a moment on my feet; Kellin was quick to steady me. I tugged on her pendulum. "Use it to find him, Kellin. Hell, use it to find any other survivors. We're...we're going to need everyone we can get." I leaned against her, knees shaking.

"How do you know?"

I deadpanned. *You have to ask, Kel? I just* know. "I haven't had a real, *bona fide* vision yet, if that's what you're asking. Then again, I think I'm still half high on fumes from cleaning supplies." *Brains are still half scrambled. Give me a good night's sleep; I'm sure I'll start seeing things again.*

She recoiled as much as she could with me leaning against her. "Right, right. Sorry."

I shook my head. "We don't have time for sorry right now. We need to start hunting. Where are the others?"

"Rory and your brother are helping bury the dead I think, though he may have hooked up with Davon to check out buildings. Jacqueline's with Leah, working with the folks that're hurt. Drew's working with some of the camps crew on shelters. Tala's scouting for food."

That's it? What about everyone else? She must've seen the question in my eyes and shook her head. "That's all we've found so far, Marin. It's not looking good."

"Apparently not." I exhaled a sigh, feeling goosebumps race up and down my arms. I shook my head. "Let's get on with this. My feet are killing me."

"After you walked all that way? Yeah, that doesn't surprise me." She let me lean on her as we made our way out from under the shelter, out into the waning light. The sullen sky roiled, clouds gathering in the west. I grimaced, watching them drift ever-so-slowly eastward, toward us, tendrils reaching across the sky. Here and there, every so often, a faint streak of light would mark them—whether rock or lightning, I couldn't be sure. Either way, they were coming. A storm was coming.

The clouds above us roiled, twisted. Thunder rumbled in the distance, though I didn't see any lightning to spark it. Rain splashed down against the weathered concrete and we huddled together, sharing blankets against the damp and the cold. Carolyn grimaced as she stretched shaking hands toward a small fire that crackled and popped, barely staying alive. She seemed to concentrate a moment, and the fire stopped struggling, strengthening a moment. Kellin nodded slowly, smiling weakly. I just shivered a little, drawing closer to whoever was next to me and listened to the rain keep coming down...

I pressed a hand against my temple, groaning quietly as I leaned a little more heavily on Kellin for a moment, letting the vision run its course and dissipate. *Bloody hell. I say something about not having any visions, and one hits me between the eyes.* There wasn't much to it and I didn't try to hang onto the vision, delve any deeper. I wanted to focus on the present, on finding survivors—especially Thom. Kellin threw a questioning glance in my direction and I just shook my head. *Don't need to worry about what I'm seeing right now. Need to worry about the here and now first.* "We'll need Drew, at least. Some of the guys from the camps could be useful, too, in case we need to carry anyone."

She grunted, then nodded in agreement. "At the very least, we'll need Drew to carry *you*."

"What's that supposed to mean? I can walk." *Maybe. Slowly. It'll hurt like a bitch and I'll be useless for a couple days, but...* She deadpanned at me and I sighed. "Fine. Park me someplace where I can watch, at least."

"Can probably do that. We'll start with what's left of Mackinac, I think, and work from there." She pulled me across the hill—I could see a few makeshift shelters of furniture taking shape, though mostly it was just a forest of beds, desks, and shelves in various states of assembly scattered across the area. The buildings looked stable enough, but I was wholly understanding of their logic—I wouldn't trust them, either, not with everything that was happening, not with the ground heaving erratically. They were giant brick tombs, especially if things shook *just* right—or just *wrong*. I knew what those floors could shake like on a normal day, let alone a day with earthquakes.

"Drew!" Kellin lifted her arm to wave.

Drew was working on hauling a wardrobe out of Robinson Hall with Jack Schmidt, one of the camp staffers. He glanced at us for a moment, blinked, then continues to help Jack haul the wardrobe out. They struggled to get it partway up the hill before they unceremoniously dropped it into the thick grass there. Drew cocked his head to one side, looking at me. His tone was half teasing, half chiding. "Up already, Marin?"

I made a rude gesture, feeling about as tired as I'm sure I looked. "Up not soon enough, apparently. We're going survivor hunting. Can't believe you hadn't thought of *that* yet."

Drew grimaced. "Most have found us. We haven't had to look."

"And the ones who can't come find us? They don't get to live?" I gave him a dirty look to match his sheepish one. In hindsight, I shouldn't have laid into him so hard. He didn't deserve that, on top of everything else that he was facing—what all of us were facing. I was worried, though, more than I was willing to admit at the time. I wanted Thom to be all right, wanted to find him. I wanted to find our other friends; I prayed silently that they were still alive, waiting for someone to come rescue them. It was all I *could* do, and that hope was all we had except each other.

Kellin sighed. "Arguing isn't going to do anyone any good. Let's go. Grab some of the camp staff, Drew. We'll check Mackinac first."

"Right." Drew looked at Jack, then the two of them headed back into Robinson Hall as Kellin and I slowly made our way over to the wreck of the Mackinac Hall complex.

The center columns that had towered above the open courtyard had come down, crushing tables and smashing windows. One corner of the building had already collapsed, and other parts were in a state of partial collapse. Most of the building's glass littered the ground and I grimaced, hoping against hope that there hadn't been too many people inside when it started to come down. Apparently, the ground wasn't nearly as stable as the contractors who'd worked on it had thought.

I sank down on what was left of a bench at the edge of the courtyard while Kellin unwound her pendulum from around her neck, wrapping a good portion of the chain around her hand. She took a deep breath, watching the finger of stone dangle from her fingertips, then glanced at me. "Wish me luck."

I smiled weakly. "You're better at it than I ever was." *Good luck, Kel.*

She grinned wryly at me, then took another deep breath, as she relaxed her hand and arm, closing her eyes a moment. She opened them again as the pendulum began to swing lazily toward the wreckage of the buildings. Moving carefully, she walked the path set out before her, following the pendulum's direction into the devastated courtyard. I watched, rubbing gently at my feet and calves, as she picked her way through the debris. Drew joined me with three of the camp staffers before to long.

"Has she found anyone yet?"

I shrugged a little. "Not sure. She hasn't said anything if she has." *Gods, please. Please let her find him alive. Please. Please just let this work.*

Then her voice called from deeper into the ruin. "Over here! I think I've found someone!"

Awakenings: Book One is available
wherever ebooks are sold.

Print release expected May 2012.

Awakenings
Book One

Erin M. Klitzke

OTHER WORKS BY ERIN M. KLITZKE

Awakenings (Book One)

Epsilon universe
Falling Stars
Epsilon: Broken Stars
Epsilon: Redeemer (forthcoming)

Lost Angels Chronicles
When All's Said and Done (forthcoming)

UNSETIC Files
Girl from a Brigadoon (forthcoming)

Non-Fiction
Intersection with the Once and Future King